SelfSame

SelfSame

By Melissa Conway

Prologue

New York Colony, 1764

"Tell me the story, Grandmother."

The old woman compressed her lips and sighed out her nose, but she placed the candlestick on the mantel and sat in the spindly wooden chair next to Enid's bed. She settled the folds of her shawl around her and took a shallow breath that rattled a little in her throat. The story had been told so many times the words came easily, even without using her native Mahican tongue. She'd learned a smattering of German from the Moravian missionaries who'd come to her village when Enid's mother was just a baby. They'd baptized the old woman with the name Elizabeth in 1743, and later she'd learned English from her son-in-law, an emigrant from Ulster, so her accent was an odd mixture of Mahican, German and Irish.

The tips of her grey braids brushed her knees as she leaned forward. The light from the fire dying in the grate sparkled in the little girl's eyes as her grandmother began.

"When yer mother birthed ye, not a breath did ye take, and yer skin were the color o' twilight."

It was an exaggeration, of course. The limp and unresponsive infant's color hadn't been nearly as dark a blue as the twilit sky, but the image was imprinted vividly in Elizabeth's memory. She hadn't seen a color quite like it in the natural world, not among the wildflowers or the deep, still ponds; not even in God's great sky.

"The German midwife thought ye had gone to God, but yer mother begged yer father to send for Bear Talker, the Muheconneok medicine man on the outskirts of the village, who had never renounced the old ways. He came, and he said *ŏtschitschaquà* – yer spirit – had departed, but mayhap could be called back. He sang the old songs, and rocked ye and rubbed ye. When ye began to cry, it seemed a miracle from the Creator. But the medicine man said no. He said ye came back but left half yer spirit in another place and time, and that yer soul were now forever *nesche* – two – and ye would have both lives to live."

Enid had snuck her thumb into her mouth but spoke around it. "Sorcha."

Elizabeth nodded solemnly and reached out to pull Enid's hand down; the thumb came out of her mouth with a little pop.

"The selfsame," Elizabeth said softly. "Give yer other grandmother me greetings when ye wake."

"I will," Enid said as her eyes began to droop.

Chapter One

Sorcha

The old oak tree had seen another summer, despite Grammy Fay's dire predictions that it would fall over onto the house any day now. Sorcha Sloane cut across the lawn and stepped over the oak's exposed roots. When she was younger, she would have made a game of it, jumping from root to gnarly root chanting, 'High diddle diddle,' but she'd long since outgrown children's games. The unseasonably warm October days and cool nights had turned the oak's leaves red, and they flickered in the light breeze like flames against the morning sky.

A blue car was idling beyond the picket fence. Sorcha could tell her ride to school hadn't been waiting long; dust from the dirt lane hung in the air. She shifted her backpack and reached to open the passenger door, but there was someone in her seat. She ducked down and looked past the interloper to Paula, whose stiff smile and raised eyebrows told her this was none of her doing. Sorcha opened the back door and shoved books, clothes and fast food wrappings aside to make room.

"What's up?" she asked after she shut the door.

Paula shifted into drive and said, "This is Luanne. Mom asked me to give her a ride today since her mom had to visit her uncle in the hospital."

The dark-haired young woman in the passenger's seat turned, revealing a slightly aquiline nose in a profile that hinted at Native American ancestry. Sorcha, who'd been prepared to dislike her for no good reason, changed her opinion when Luanne said dryly, "He's actually in jail."

There were less than four hundred students at Sorcha's high school and as far as she knew, Luanne wasn't one of them. "You go to PFH?"

Luanne snorted. "Not anymore. I'm twenty-two. I just need a ride to the bus station." After a short pause: "I'm in college."

"What's your major?" Paula asked. They were on the main road now, a nearly treeless stretch of farmland a few miles from town.

"Anthropology. Native American studies."

Sorcha leaned forward. "Are you Muheconneok? I mean, Mohican?"

"Iroquois." Luanne twisted in her seat and looked at Sorcha intently. "You?"

The question surprised her a little. With her white skin and reddish-brown hair, Sorcha looked nothing like a Native American.

"Oh…um, not really," she said. "We think my however-many-greats grandmother was half Mohican, though."

She saw Paula's blue eyes shift in the rearview mirror but ignored the warning look. It wasn't as if she was about to burst out with the truth.

"Ah," Luanne said. "They say every American has a drop of native blood. Are you interested in genealogy and antiques? Or architecture? Because your house is awesome. How old is it?"

Paula was still staring at her in the rearview mirror, so Sorcha tapped her lightly on the shoulder and muttered, "Watch the road," before looking back at Luanne's avidly interested face. She knew Luanne was just curious and it couldn't hurt to answer her questions, but she had become so adept at deflection the response came automatically. She shrugged and said, "I don't know."

It wasn't true; she knew exactly how old the house was. The stone walls and floors of the main rooms had been built in 1757 in the modified Dutch Colonial style that was popular in the Hudson River Valley at the time. Over the course of the next two and a half centuries, the house had undergone many changes and additions. It had been drafty and creaky when it had been new, and it was drafty and creaky now.

Luanne's face fell. She made a disappointed tsk sound and turned to face forward as if she'd lost interest in anything else Sorcha had to say.

Paula, apparently in an attempt to change a subject that had already expired, said, "Luanne is Ben Webster's big sister."

It took Sorcha a second to realize who Paula meant. Ben had been a year ahead of them in school, so she hadn't ever really gotten to know him. She did know that two years ago he'd been busted for assault and sent away to juvie. She'd heard several versions of the story; that Ben was defending himself; that he was defending another kid; that he'd attacked unprovoked – but in each version the story had the same ending: he'd kicked the crap out of his opponent.

She hadn't heard he was back, but he'd be a senior this year anyway and since she and Paula were juniors, they wouldn't have any of the same classes with him.

She wasn't sure how sensitive the subject was with Luanne, so she went with a noncommittal, "Oh, yeah?"

She needn't have worried. Luanne scoffed and said, "Yeah, my delinquent little bro is back. At least that's what everyone says. Juvenile Hall is supposed to set kids on the straight and narrow, but all it does is teach them how to be criminals just to survive the experience."

Yeesh. Sorcha made a mental note to avoid Ben Webster.

Paula turned onto the Town Center exit. "I saw him on Friday. He looks normal."

Luanne sighed. "He may not be covered in homemade tats, but he's having a hard time reintegrating. He's been…fine, I guess. But not the same. Angrier. The system let him down."

Paula double-parked in front of the bus station and Luanne jumped out. She leaned her head in the open door to say quickly, "Thanks – and sorry about the rant," before slamming it shut and walking away.

Sorcha climbed between the seats to sit up front. "That was awkward."

Paula shrugged as she pulled back onto Main Street, but flashed a toothy grin and said, "Wait 'til you see him. He's a drop-dead hottie."

Sorcha aimed a disbelieving look at her friend. "Are you serious? Didn't you hear her? Even his own sister thinks he's toxic."

"I didn't say I was gonna marry him! Just that he's hot. Too hot to give me the time of day anyway."

Sorcha frowned, wondering if Paula's fluctuating self-esteem was headed for another low. She'd gotten a tan over the summer, which helped clear up the worst of her acne, but she'd also gained ten pounds and outgrown most of her clothes. Neither of the girls came from wealthy families and shopping for outfits at the local Salvation Army was only cool if you could afford not to. Paula's parents were divorced, and her mom worked from home as a medical transcriber, which is why Paula got to drive the car.

"Whatever," Sorcha said. "He's a loser. And your hair still looks great, by the way."

Paula's mom had taken her into the city to get her dishwater-blonde hair streaked and cut as a special surprise. The stylist had worked miracles on her formerly untamed mane and now it hung in a smooth and shining bob below her ears. The cut had gone a long way to starting the year off on a positive note for Sorcha's best friend.

Paula flipped her hair back and batted her eyelashes. "It does, doesn't it?"

She drove onto the field adjacent to the school and stopped next to a jacked-up black truck. They got out and wove their way through the cars whose drivers hadn't gotten there early enough to secure one of the few spots designated for students in the paved lot.

Preston Field High, derisively referred to by the sound '*pfh*,' was a sprawling brick complex built back in the 1960's. Principal Kessler was a paranoid former inner-city teacher who used some unusual methods to keep his students motivated. While other schools had done away with lockers completely, Principal Kessler allowed students with a 'B' average or better to have them. It was supposed to be some kind of motivational tool, as if the higher achievers were less likely to abuse the privilege by storing guns or drugs in them.

Sorcha and Paula both earned a locker this year, but they shared Sorcha's while Paula rented hers out to a kid with a B-minus average for ten bucks a month. Paula was always looking for ways to make extra cash and was a very popular babysitter.

At their locker, Sorcha said, "So did Luanne give you gas money or anything?"

Paula shook her head. "They're barely scraping by since their dad was killed in Afghanistan."

"That's terrible," Sorcha murmured, but the bell put an end to the conversation.

At lunch, they met up in the cafeteria, which was also the auditorium and gymnasium. For the third year in a row, they'd claimed their usual spot sitting cross-legged on the narrow portion of the stage nearest the left-side stairs, affording them a great view of the room while giving them semi-privacy at the same time. Sorcha had barely sat down and begun rooting around in her sack lunch when Paula hissed, "There he is!"

Reflexively, Sorcha looked up. A tall young man with shoulder-length black hair was walking up the center aisle between tables, carrying a tray of food. He was dressed in jeans, tennis shoes and a plain blue t-shirt and didn't look dangerous or unstable at all. She'd seen him a few times and wondered who he was and had to agree with Paula's assessment that he was good-looking. He had a less feminine version of his sister's nose and big brown eyes under rather heavy straight brows.

Sorcha watched surreptitiously as he scanned the room until an arm belonging to a boy at the table directly in front of them shot up and waved him over. He sat facing the boy, and coincidentally facing Sorcha as well. She looked away before any accidental eye contact occurred and then, for good measure, scooted her butt around until she was sitting sideways towards Paula.

Paula gave her an incredulous look and said quietly, "Afraid he's gonna give you cooties all the way over here?"

6

Sorcha lifted her shoulders defensively. "Eat your lunch."

She bit into her salami and lettuce sandwich and chewed self-consciously, telling herself that Ben Webster was not watching her.

"Um, I think he's checking you out," Paula whispered.

"Shut up!" Sorcha whispered back. Her stomach burned and the sandwich suddenly tasted like cardboard. She wrapped it up hastily and shoved it back in the bag, sitting there feeling like she was on display – just like she'd felt so recently and yet so long ago.

"Oh, crap," Paula said, putting a hand on Sorcha's knee. "I'm sorry. Are you okay?"

Sorcha swallowed bile but nodded.

"Did anything happen that you want to tell me about?" Paula asked.

Sorcha closed her eyes for a brief moment, but saw the earnest, ugly face of Jedediah Johnson and opened them again. "We're betrothed."

"Gross," Paula breathed. "What are you gonna do?"

Sorcha gave her best friend a grim smile and looked at her with brimming eyes. "Endure it."

When she got home that afternoon, she dropped her backpack on the kitchen table and went out the back door. Grammy Fay was on her knees weeding a patch of winter squash. The old woman looked up from under her wide-brimmed hat and waved a gloved hand absently as Sorcha wandered to the wrought-iron gate set in the center of the big yard's cinder-brick fence. Beyond the yard, on the northern slope of the thirty-two acres of land owned by her father, was the family cemetery. It was a familiar, comforting walk in the warm afternoon sun. There were sixty-four gravestones, the oldest dating back to 1784, but a few had no death date inscribed on them, so it was impossible to tell how old they were. The last person to be buried there was Sorcha's great-great grandfather. After that, cremation became popular, so the cemetery went out of use.

Sorcha settled on the stone retaining wall and looked out over the sea of mottled grey stones. Most stood upright as they should, but some were askew or broken or knocked down altogether. The graveyard was well tended; her father kept the grass trim and wildflowers were encouraged to grow. She knew the name and history of almost every person buried there. She'd denied being interested in genealogy when Luanne asked, but that was another lie. Her ancestors were a very specific concern of hers and she'd been gathering information on them since she was old enough to read. She'd traced her line back as far as the beginning of the nineteenth century, but all the birth records in the village prior to that had been destroyed when the old church burned to the ground.

One person she was especially interested in was not buried here, nor had Sorcha ever been able to find a record of her death, no matter how desperately she'd searched.

Chapter Two

Enid

Sorcha lay down in bed that night and stared at the glowing red numbers of her alarm clock. She never set the alarm to go off because it wouldn't wake her if it did. When she was born, she'd been kept in the hospital for weeks because unlike other infants who woke, ate and slept at regular – and normal – intervals, she slept twelve hours a day and then was awake for twelve hours. The doctors diagnosed her with a sleeping disorder, an aberrant form of hypersomnia, but without the excessive daytime sleepiness that normally went along with it. All her parents knew was her tiny body refused to stir until some inner alarm clock went off, and then their child was alert and refreshed and never, ever took a nap during the day.

When she was old enough to speak, she'd talked about another world – another life she lived while she was asleep in this one. At first her parents indulged her 'imaginary friend,' but over the course of time, it became clear to them that this was no ordinary fantasy. Her 'obsession' earned her years of intensive therapy until she recognized the need to keep Enid secret in Sorcha's world and, lest she be labeled a witch, Sorcha secret in Enid's. Only her grandmothers, Elizabeth then and Fay now, knew and believed. And Paula, of course, but Sorcha sometimes wondered if Paula was only humoring her. Sorcha had no proof other than her uncanny knowledge of daily life in the eighteenth century, something she couldn't have researched at the age of six, when she first told Paula the truth.

She lay in bed, stalling; something she daren't do. Enid must get up on time and begin her daily chores, or there'd be hell to pay. But Sorcha didn't want to go. Not if it meant facing that vile man who was about to own her, body and…well, he didn't know it, but he was only getting half her soul.

Her eyelids were heavy, her body ready for sleep. She knew that moments after she dozed, she'd be there…

9

Her eyes opened again. Light filtered through the dusty window coverings. It was cold in the room and warm under the covers, but Enid didn't dawdle. She knew she was late.

After quickly using the chamber pot and splashing her face with frigid water from the bucket in the corner, she pulled on her stockings and struggled into her stays, silently cursing the endless layers of clothing required for common decency in the eighteenth century. Her one good under petticoat needed washing, but there was nothing she could do about it now. She finished dressing and tucked her hair into her white linen cap, wishing for the millionth time she could shower every day like Sorcha. But bathing was frowned upon by the superstitious village folk, besides being an unheard-of luxury for a poor farmer's daughter.

Enid quickly checked on her grandmother, who was snoring lightly in her bed. Downstairs in the kitchen, her father was sitting at the table with a wooden cup held loosely in his hand. The stench of sour cider filled the room. He looked up, face expressionless, and said, "Ye'll be leavin' on the morrow."

Enid nodded and went straight to the fire to retrieve the pot of porridge that had been cooking slowly in the embers all night. She served her father a bowl without looking directly at him. She always saw her mother reflected in his cold blue eyes, saw him flinch a little when he looked at her, as if every glimpse of Enid's face forced him to relive his wife's abandonment all over again.

She looked just like her mother, or so she was told; she'd been four when her mother left. There were no mirrors in the house, but Enid had studied her heart-shaped face and deep-set eyes in the window glass. She and Sorcha looked nothing alike. Enid had nearly black hair to Sorcha's reddish-brown, and her eyes were the color of mud, whereas Sorcha's were a deep-sea green. Enid wasn't pretty by Sorcha's standards, but in the lower classes in this day and age it was best to be plain so you didn't attract unwanted attention.

Enid didn't know why her mother left; whether her father's cruelty had driven her away or if he had become broken and bitter because of her departure. She only knew her mother had been there one day and was gone the next, leaving behind her husband, young half-breed daughter and her old mother, now called Elizabeth. Grandmother Elizabeth once told her that her mother, whose Mahican name was Bluebird, had pined for the old ways and went to live with the Iroquois in the south, but it wasn't a subject they often discussed in that house.

Aggie, the new household slave, entered from the side door carrying a full bucket of milk. A basket of eggs was nestled in the crook of her other arm. Her black eyes warily watched Fergus Thompson's back as she skirted behind him to set the bucket on the floor next to the churn. She set the basket on the buffet table and then tried to leave quietly the way she'd come, but Fergus reached back without looking and snagged her skirt. The dusky-skinned girl didn't resist as he pulled her to his side.

Enid busied herself readying the brick oven for baking, trying to ignore Aggie's murmured sounds of protest at whatever her father was doing. Aggie was the former slave of Jedediah Johnson, who'd given her to Fergus in what Enid suspected was trade for his daughter. She tried to console herself that unlike Aggie, at least she was getting marriage out of the deal. She was only a year older than Aggie and had no idea what the other girl thought about her new situation. She did know how lonely her father had been, but seeing him with a girl half his age, and from the sound of it, a girl very much unwilling, made her sick.

Despite the fact that it would probably anger him, she abruptly left the room, left the house. She rushed past the young oak tree and headed for the orchard by the creek. Plucking an apple from the nearest branch, she stalked to her favorite patch of meadow and flounced down in the light of the rising sun. The grass was moist with dew, but not wet enough to soak through her skirts. She was hungry and the apple was crisp and sweet, but she hardly enjoyed it.

Not for the first time, she railed internally against the disparity between her world and Sorcha's. In her innermost mind, she and Sorcha were one and the same person, but on the outside, out of necessity, she'd developed two distinct personalities. Both lives were hers, but they were wildly divergent, and she much preferred life in the twenty-first century. How could she not? Here, she was slightly better than a slave, working from sunup to sundown with very little joy in her life. There, slavery no longer existed! At least not in America. Aggie was in the kitchen right now sitting on Enid's father's lap, unable to stop him from fondling her. Enid certainly couldn't help her. Sorcha's father wouldn't dream of doing such a thing, but if he did, Sorcha wouldn't be completely helpless. Here, the authorities would laugh if Enid tried to tell them; then her father would beat her and it would all be legal and normal.

She got up and fetched a bucket, filling it quickly with apples that hung low on the branches. Her father would forgive her lapse in manners for storming out of the kitchen if she used the excuse that she planned to bake him a cobbler.

Before she reached the front door, she heard the dull *clop clop* of a horse's hooves on the dirt track. She stepped a little faster, hoping to get inside before the visitor got near enough to see her, but then, "Miss Thompson!" rang out. Enid shuddered, because of course it was Jedediah.

Resigned, she turned and offered him the best smile she could muster. No matter how odious his appearance, no matter that his first wife was barely cold in her grave; he would give her a respectable home, and that was more than the daughter of a poor Irish immigrant and a Mohican squaw could hope for.

"Good day to you, Mr. Johnson."

Jedediah's bay mare rolled her eyes and snorted, bucking a little as he dismounted. "This one," he said, stroking the mare's neck and then giving it a firm pat, "is a spirited animal. Can ya ride?"

Enid had ridden the nag that pulled her father's plow many times. "Yes, sir."

"Have ya ever ridden for sport?"

She blinked. "Forgive me, sir, but do you mean hunting?"

Jedediah laughed. His teeth were stained brown and some were black with rot, and his Adam's apple bobbed on his thin neck. "No, my dear girl, I mean for pleasure. Have ya ever ridden for the sheer joy of it?"

A rare memory of her mother chose that moment to surface: Enid, looking across a wide, sunny field of young corn from the bare back of a spotted pony; a woman with two black braids hanging down her back, gazing over her shoulder at Enid, brown eyes crinkled in laughter.

She looked down at her feet. "No, sir."

"Jedediah!" Her father's voice boomed from the doorway. "I see ye've come to look over yer property. Pray reassure me there be no buyer's remorse!"

Enid had to give it to Jedediah: he looked appalled at Fergus' crudeness. "Not at all," he said. "I were merely passin' by."

"On the way to where?" Fergus asked, gesturing at the wilderness encroaching on the farm.

Jedediah's face went red and Enid took pity on him. "It is a lovely morning for a ride."

"Yes…yes! Would that ya could accompany me." He looked expectantly at Fergus.

Her father's face froze, but only for an instant. Social convention didn't mean much on the edge of the frontier, not to someone like Fergus. He said gruffly, "Take her," before turning on his heel and stomping back into the house.

Enid sat behind Jedediah's saddle, balanced precariously on the mare's wide rump. If she could have gotten away with it, she would have straddled the mare instead of sitting with both legs primly to the side. As it was, she had to hold tight to Jedediah's waist to prevent her heels from digging into the skittish mare's hindquarters.

As expected, Jedediah smelled horrible. No one ever washed and because of it, the stink of human body odor was commonplace. It was one of many things Sorcha found distasteful that Enid had to tolerate. She reached a hand into her linen dress and wiggled her fingers under the waistband of her petticoat. There, she dug deep into the pocket tied around her waist and withdrew a small bundle. Pressing it tightly against her nose, she inhaled the dried lavender within.

Jedediah said, "I know the weddin' is sudden-like for ya. I thought mebbe ya'd like to see the farm."

"That would be a comfort, I am sure," Enid replied.

He didn't talk much after that. Her father's farm was on the outskirts of the village to the west of them. They rode east, away from what little civilization the area offered. The mare plodded along the narrow trail, past a placid pond, which even in her apprehension Enid found beautiful. When they finally reached Jedediah's homestead, the sun was high in the clear October sky.

To say her father had told her little about what to expect would have been an understatement. The house was a log cabin built precariously atop a steeply rising hill. Each jerking step the mare took threatened to unseat Enid. She was forced to clutch Jedediah even more closely as they lurched upward. He'd scratched at his scalp several times on the trip; she prayed his greasy hair was not infested with lice.

Next to the house was a small chicken coop, the only other structure in sight. She heard the clucking of chickens, but no lowing of cows. A scan of the area didn't reveal a recognizable crop. She'd assumed he was a farmer since he'd called this a farm, but there was no evidence of it. From the looks of the house, he wasn't a carpenter. In this day and age, it would the height of discourtesy to ask him what his occupation was, even if she was about to marry him.

When they approached the front entrance to the cabin, a middle-aged black woman appeared with two white children clutching her apron. Jedediah dismounted and helped Enid from the back of his horse. The children didn't move; didn't rush forward yelling, "Daddy!" But Enid knew they were his, and the discovery made her already nervous stomach cramp up something fierce.

The next hour passed in a blur. Inside, the rough-hewn walls and floor spoke volumes about Jedediah's lack of prosperity. He was a poor man trying to hack a living out of the wilderness. Poorer even than Fergus, despite the fact that he owned a slave. But however deprived the household, it was well-kept by Bess, whose resemblance to Aggie suggested she was the slave girl's mother. The children were Sarah and Ezekiel, six and five years old respectively. Neither one looked at her with curiosity. They knew she was to be their new mother, but their faces were blank, and their demeanor subdued. Enid knew very little about children but was intuitive enough to see they were in shock. She could certainly relate. The one window in the main room was open to the afternoon air, and either by design or accident it framed the view of a lone headstone about a hundred yards behind the cabin.

By the time Jedediah dropped her off in front of her father's house, she longed to go to sleep and live in Sorcha's world again.

Chapter Three

Sorcha

It had become habit to wake up and immediately construct a mental barrier between her worlds in order to function normally each day. When she spoke about Enid to Paula or her grandmother, she acted as if she were talking about another person. Disassociating herself made it easier to cope.

This morning, she found it harder than usual to push her raw emotions behind the barrier. She took an extra-long shower, scrubbing her skin pink as if it would banish the persistent memory of Jedediah's stench.

After she got dressed in a short-sleeved white sweater and skinny jeans that tucked into her furry-edged ankle boots, she wanted nothing more than to rush out into the countryside and locate Jedediah's cabin, but it had been so rickety she doubted the structure still existed. The gravestone that she'd assumed belonged to Jedediah's dead wife might or might not still be there – her coffin could have been removed and placed elsewhere by new property owners at any time in the last 240 years. Or her final resting place could have merely been reclaimed by the land, obliterated from all memory.

Sorcha poured herself a bowl of raisin bran and slurped it down in her father's study while she researched the property online. She was pretty sure she already knew what she would find, and sure enough, county records showed the entire area had been developed as condos.

Grammy Fay poked her head in. Her salt-and-pepper hair was still in curlers, but she was dressed in one of her favorite velour tracksuits. "What are you up to, young lady?"

Sorcha had a mouthful of cereal and couldn't answer fast enough to stop Fay from jumping to her own conclusion. "Do I interpret your silence to mean you don't want to tell me? I hope you're not still trying to find out when Enid died."

It was a source of constant conflict between them. Fay was firm in her conviction that Sorcha would have no end of trouble getting on with her lives if she knew when she, as Enid, was going to die.

Sorcha replied testily, "I know, I know. It's perverse of me, but I can't help it. I have to know."

Fay had emigrated from Ireland as a child and had deep ties to Celtic mythology. Sorcha fully expected a superstitious piece of wisdom and Fay didn't disappoint. "It's dangerous to tempt fate."

Sorcha nodded. "That's what Elizabeth says, too."

Enid's grandmother was just as superstitious as Fay; it was something else the two old women had in common.

"How is she?"

Sorcha looked up. "Not well."

Elizabeth's grave was in the family cemetery out back. Her small, weatherworn tombstone was inscribed, 'Elizabeth, b. 1700. Beloved Grandmother." It was obvious from the words that Enid had not only composed them, but deliberately left off Elizabeth's date of death, thus preventing herself, as Sorcha, from finding out when her grandmother would die. From Elizabeth's long-standing symptoms, Sorcha knew she probably had tuberculosis and it was only a matter of time.

In a mock-cheerful voice, she said, "And Enid's about to be married off to a freshly-widowed farmer, so I don't know what will happen to Elizabeth after she moves out."

Fay gasped. "What? Why didn't you say anything? Married?"

"Yes, Grammy, married. It's a common occurrence in the colonies for teenagers to marry. We don't have much choice in the matter. No one gives a crap about all the pervy old men hooking up with little girls."

"He's old? Who is he? Do you like him at all?"

With a monumental effort, Sorcha kept her face neutral. If her true feelings showed, Fay would worry, and when Fay worried, she forced Sorcha to think and talk about Enid's life. "He could be worse."

"Oh." Fay sounded doubtful.

Sorcha powered her father's computer off and stood. To forestall what she anticipated was coming next, she said, "I know all about the birds and bees, Grammy."

Fay's hand slowly rose to cover her mouth. She stared at her granddaughter with eloquent eyes.

Sorcha brushed past her and grabbed her backpack. Outside, a crisp white frost covered the lawn. She thought about going back inside for a jacket but didn't want her grandmother to get her second wind, and besides, Paula was waiting in the lane.

With Luanne in the passenger seat. Again. Sighing, Sorcha got into the back.

Luanne turned and grinned, revealing a slight gap between her front teeth Sorcha hadn't noticed before. "Sorry to disrupt the carpool routine again. Bail was set a bit rich for Mom's blood, so she had to go visit her cousin in Poughkeepsie. He's a bondsman."

Sorcha didn't mean to be rude, but she was tense and irritated, so she didn't pause to consider the question that popped out, "How does Ben get to school?" *And why aren't you riding with him?*

Luanne didn't seem to be offended. "He rides his bike."

"Every day?" Paula asked. "That's a long ride from Cliffside."

Luanne nodded. "Yeah. He's kinda hard-core."

"So that's how he got that gluteus maximus."

Paula's comment made Sorcha roll her eyes, but Luanne only laughed and said, "Mountain biking'll do that to a butt."

Sorcha didn't want to talk about Ben Webster – she couldn't help but compare him to Jedediah. She dug her smartphone out and accessed Google maps, trying to ignore it as her best friend rather unsubtly probed Luanne for more information on Ben. She pulled up the satellite map of the general area where Jedediah's cabin was once located. A little north of the condo development was what looked to be a park, but there was a small separate building, too.

"Whatcha doin'?" Luanne asked. Sorcha looked up to find the older girl's eyes fixed on her smartphone.

"Nothing."

Before Sorcha realized her intention, Luanne plucked the phone out of her hand and examined it closely. "That used to be the old Native American Artifacts Exhibition. Standard second grade field trip." She handed the phone back.

"Oh, yeah," Paula said. "Remember, Sorch, in Mrs. Beckett's class? Mario Sanchez knocked over that stuffed horse display?"

How could she forget? She'd been standing ten feet away when the horse came crashing down and split open, spewing moldy sawdust all over her.

"The museum," she said thoughtfully. Even as a second-grader Sorcha had recognized the Native American Artifacts Exhibition for what it was: a small, low-budget, under-staffed local showcase. Maybe someone there knew something about the history of the area, though.

"We live nearby but it's closed now," Luanne said, unintentionally dashing Sorcha's hopes. "The old guy who ran the place donated all the items to my college and we built a whole wing dedicated to the area's history."

She said 'we' like she had something to do with whatever rich benefactor got a tax deduction from building that wing.

Luanne rambled on. "There's some really rare stuff, some of it from as far back as the American Revolution...but I'm sure you're not interested."

Sorcha produced a polite smile designed to throw Luanne off the fact that she *was* interested. Enid had been born in the midst of the French and Indian War, and even though history showed her small village played no part in the events of that war, Sorcha knew it had affected many of the villager's lives – *taken* many of their lives. She tried to learn all she could to keep Enid and Elizabeth safe now that the conflict between the colonials and loyalists was heating up, but it wasn't easy finding useful information. Written history in general was so condensed; limited to events the powers-that-be at the time considered important enough to record for posterity, and those events were often filtered or censored by whoever recorded it. Sometimes she stumbled across transcribed diaries or letters on the Internet, but none thus far had touched upon Enid's isolated village. The same village Paula drove through now.

After Paula dropped Luanne at the bus stop, Sorcha climbed into the front seat and said, "'Gluteus maximus?' Seriously?"

Paula laughed and said, "Shut up."

"No, really," Sorcha persisted. "What happened to your undying love for Dalton Boyle?"

It was the crush to end all crushes. Four long years Paula had pined for the boy next door. It drove Sorcha crazy that instead of trying to get to know him, Paula bolted in the opposite direction whenever she saw him. Her excuse was that she was terrified of making a fool of herself, but Sorcha secretly thought Paula was afraid she'd find out the real Dalton didn't measure up to the one who'd lived so long in her fantasies. Having spoken to him on more than one occasion, Sorcha was pretty sure he couldn't possibly.

"I'm infatuated, not dead," Paula replied.

The rest of the morning felt like a déjà vu of the day before. Usually, she preferred Sorcha's life, but today her classes, teachers and classmates were all filler serving as a minor distraction from her dark thoughts of Enid's future. She was wholly focused on the problem of locating the site of Jedediah's cabin, and by lunchtime, had resolved to visit the area in person. For that, she needed transportation.

At lunch, Paula joined her on the stage and flipped the latch on her Little Kitty lunchbox. As she went to work spreading soft cheese on a cracker, Sorcha debated how to go about convincing her to go on a field trip. Tentatively, she asked, "So what are you doing after school?"

"Today?" Paula said through a mouthful of cracker.

"No, in the year 2525. Yes, today."

Paula shrugged, but then her brows wrinkled. "You need a ride?"

Sorcha nodded.

Paula took a swig of her strawberry milk, burped delicately and said, "Where we going? Native American museum?"

"Is that alright?"

"Luanne said it was closed. You planning on breaking in?"

Sorcha looked away without answering. Ben Webster was sitting in the same spot as yesterday, but there were two new faces at his table – both girls who appeared to be hanging on his every word. With the girls' flirtatious smiles to look at, there was no danger of him glancing up and catching her eye, so she studied him. His left eyebrow kept disappearing into the lock of dark hair curving across his forehead, but otherwise, his face was nearly expressionless. There was something about the way he moved his head when he spoke, however, that told her how much he was enjoying the attention. Probably hadn't hung out with many females in the two years he'd been incarcerated at juvenile hall.

"Earth to Sorch," Paula said. "Come in, Sorch."

Sorcha let out a small laugh and looked back at her friend. As if the last minute or so hadn't passed without a response, she said, "No I don't want to break in. Just look around a little."

Paula shrugged again. "Your wish is my command."

They were late getting started because Paula had a little accident in Art, her last class of the day. Apparently, someone found it amusing to set an open tube of acrylic paint on her chair and she'd sat on it, squirting Thalo Blue all down her jeans. Sorcha helped her rinse the worst of it out in the bathroom sink.

"Who did it?" she asked.

Paula snorted. "Dunno, but Kristin Barber sure thought it was funny."

"She's just jealous because you can paint circles around her."

"I'd like to paint a circle around her – with a pentagram in it. Send her back to the dimension from whence she came."

Kristin had moved to the area from California two years ago and quickly established herself as the reigning Popular Girl complete with bitchy reputation – destined to crush her competition under stiletto heels on the path to obtaining the Homecoming crown. Sorcha and Paula secretly referred to her and her cronies as the Cliché Clique because there was one in

19

every school. For Sorcha and Paula, though, Kristin and her friends were like mosquitos, easily brushed off and forgotten.

On the drive, Sorcha briefly filled Paula in on Enid's day trip to Jedediah's cabin. Paula knew better than to ask many questions afterward, and they fell into a pensive silence as the countryside flew by. Sorcha gazed out the window at the bright fall foliage, thinking that any day now the trees would be bare and the ground frozen solid. A lone bicyclist on the dirt path paralleling the highway caught her eye as he hit a mound at full speed and launched into the air. His backpack lifted off his back and slammed back down as he nailed the landing. She saw his face, bright with victory. *Ben.*

She turned away and studied the terrain as they drove onto the exit leading to Cliffside condominiums. They'd been built right up against the steeply rising hill where Jedediah's cabin once sat. The Native American Artifact Exhibition building was located at the far eastern edge of the property, on a strip of ungroomed grass and trees that contrasted sharply with the neatly trimmed patches of landscaping between each condo unit.

Paula parked on the side of the road and they got out of the car and approached the small abandoned building. Cans, bottles and cigarette butts littered the area, testimony to its popularity as a party place.

Sorcha paced up the wooden ramp and tried the door. Locked. The two tiny windows on either side had been boarded up. They walked around the whole building, but it was tightly sealed against intruders.

"What did you expect to find?" Paula asked.

Sorcha frowned. "Nothing, I guess. Thought I'd check just in case. That's where I really wanted to go." She pointed to a thin, overgrown path that led away from the museum, up the rocky slope, and disappeared somewhere behind the condos.

"You don't want to go up there." The voice came from behind and both girls whirled around. Ben stood there, shoulder-length hair blown back from the wind of his bike ride.

"Why not?" Sorcha met his eyes, challenging.

"Well, it's private property for one thing. Plus, there's a homeless old Native American dude who camps out up there every winter."

The girls exchanged a startled look before Sorcha turned back and lifted her chin. "How do you know?"

"He's my uncle."

"I thought your uncle was in jail," Paula said.

"Different uncle." His head tilted to the side. "Oh, hey, you're Paula, right? You gave Loony a ride this morning."

'Loony' must be his sister Luanne's nickname. "Yeah," Paula said. "This is Sorcha."

20

Ben's dark eyes lingered on Sorcha's face for only a moment. He didn't say anything; just pushed his bike over to the museum entrance ramp, wrapped the chain around one of the posts and clicked the lock. With his backpack slung over one shoulder, he strode past them up the narrow path. He'd walked ten yards or so before looking back. "You coming?"

Sorcha and Paula exchanged another look, more alarmed than the first, but Sorcha couldn't afford to hesitate. She followed him, skipping a little to catch up. Paula brought up the rear.

Ben didn't chit-chat on the hike up the rocky hillside and for that Sorcha was grateful. The déjà vu she'd been plagued with all day was back in full force. Her surroundings were far from identical, but her inner perspective kept shifting to Enid's memories of the ride on Jedediah's mare; the jolting and the odors and the apprehension. When they reached the top, Ben turned to her and that eyebrow of his disappeared into his hair.

"You okay?"

She consciously relaxed her face, knowing she'd been sneering in distaste at the memory of being close to Jedediah. "Yeah, fine."

"You look like you're gonna yak."

Sorcha felt Paula's hand on her shoulder, but she shrugged it off and moved past Ben to stare at the landscape. Her feet moved practically of their own accord, one step after another until she was standing where the cabin had been. In her mind's eye, she saw the headstone through the window.

In her peripheral consciousness, she heard Ben ask Paula, "What's she looking at?"

There was nothing to look at: the ground was completely bare, not even an outline of the cabin's frame remained. Sorcha walked on, straight through the invisible walls out across the rocky, packed dirt with its patches of dying grass. When she reached the place where the headstone had been, she began kicking at the ground with the toe of her boot.

"What the hell's going on?" Ben asked. "Sorcha."

It was the first time he'd said her name and for some reason it broke through her trance. She looked at him and took a deep breath that came out in a heavy sigh. "I'm searching for a gravestone."

His head went back in surprise. Paula shot her a warning look.

Ben spread his hands as his lips twisted in a sardonic smile. "I've lived here my whole life and haven't ever seen a gravestone. If you want, we can ask my Uncle Harry. He's gotta be around here somewhere."

Disappointment swept over her. "It was stupid to come here," she said. "Let's go."

She stalked past Ben and Paula on numb legs, only her determination and the steepness of the path compelling her forward.

Chapter Four

Enid

The transition from sleep to wakefulness was as seamless as ever, with one exception: Enid's morning was marred by the sensation of being shaken roughly. Her eyes opened to Aggie's worried face and the words, "Wake up, Miss. Wake up!"

Enid pushed the slave girl away and sat upright. "What is it?"

"Ye wouldn't wake. It's like ye was dead!"

"Yes, yes. I wake when I wake, and you'd do well to remember that." Enid spoke more sharply than she intended, but Aggie's urgency curled her empty stomach into a ball of dread. "What's wrong?"

"Yer father, Miss. Soldiers came to the door last night and took him off! And the old lady – she's in a bad way."

Enid threw the covers back and rushed out of the room, her bare feet thumping down the narrow hallway to Elizabeth's small room. Her grandmother was in bed, but her upper body was hanging halfway off the straw mattress, face down. For a horrified moment, Enid thought she was dead, but then her frail body began to shake as she coughed. A thin drizzle of crimson spittle hovered over the already bloodstained wooden floor. Elizabeth was feebly gasping for breath between each cough.

Enid did what she always did when her grandmother was taken by a fit. She snatched her homemade cotton face mask from the mantle and quickly fastened it over her nose and mouth. The fire had died down; she tossed a log and some sticks on and added water to the kettle that normally filled the room with steam. The bottle of medicinal elixir she'd concocted from honey mead and herbs from the garden was almost empty, but she lifted Elizabeth's torso, wiped her mouth with the bed sheet, and coaxed her into drinking the rest of it.

Enid supported her grandmother as her painfully thin body contracted into another spasm, patting her on the back to encourage the phlegm to rise. Elizabeth's nightgown and bedclothes were soaked from night sweats and Enid barked at Aggie to get fresh linens while she gently removed the soiled garments. With the slave girl's help, she managed to make her grandmother as comfortable as she could.

"Thank you, Aggie," she said. "I'm sorry I was cross."

Aggie's dark eyes dropped to the floor as she backed out of the room. "Yes, Miss."

Enid settled into the spindly chair next to the bed, the same chair Elizabeth had sat in when Enid was a child demanding to hear the story of her birth.

"It's time," Elizabeth said in a weak voice.

"Don't talk," Enid replied, fearful another coughing fit would result.

"Send for him now."

Enid assumed she meant the pastor and her eyes filled with tears. She stood, but Elizabeth's skeletal fingers reached for her. Enid took her grandmother's hand between her own and held it to her breast, waiting. The whites of Elizabeth's eyes were tinted yellow with streaks of red from vessels that had burst from the force of her coughing.

"Bear Talker," she whispered. "Bring the medicine man."

It was the last thing Enid expected her to say. Elizabeth had lived out the second half of her life as a devout Christian and was very involved with the church. Enid would have questioned her, but her grandmother fell into a doze, probably induced by the medicine Enid had learned how to make off the Internet in Sorcha's world. She'd wanted to grow her own batch of mold to use as an antibiotic to cure the tuberculosis, but the process was far too advanced for the instruments available to her in the eighteenth century. All she'd been able to do was extend her grandmother's life and make her more comfortable as she wasted away.

She went to her room and dressed as quickly as she could. Downstairs, Aggie handed her a bowl of porridge that she ate without tasting. Everyone knew the old medicine man lived in a longhouse outside the village. He was tolerated because he grew particularly fine tobacco in a secret location and traded it to the men for food and necessities.

"Who were the soldiers who took my father?" she asked.

Aggie shook her head. "I don't know, Miss."

"How many were there? What color were their uniforms?"

"Four, all on horseback, and they was dressed as men always is. They was muhlitia."

"Militia?"

At Aggie's nod, Enid looked for her father's long rifle, normally mounted above the back door. It was gone.

23

She dropped her head in her hands. "This is bad."

She wasn't worried about him; her father wasn't due to die for another decade. He was a staunch supporter of the rebellion and she knew from historical records that he would serve in several Revolutionary War campaigns – including the Battle of White Plains almost one hundred miles to the south, which, now that she thought about it, was going to happen any day now. In the back of her mind, she'd known this was coming, but thought her father would have at least prepared her for his leaving. Perhaps the local militia had coerced him into leaving so suddenly. It wasn't as if he could wake her to tell her he was going, nor could he leave her a note: he could not read or write.

"Miss, I hear them say they was headed out to Mr. Jedediah's place."

"Did they take the horse?" She didn't wait for an answer, but immediately muttered, "Of course they did."

She hastily finished her porridge. She would be forced to walk to fetch the medicine man, but given her father's lack of sympathy towards Elizabeth's illness, she would likely have had to walk whether the horse was here or not. Her father had accepted her grandmother's presence only as long as the old woman had been useful. Elizabeth had long contributed to the household income with sales of her beautiful beadwork.

Enid wrapped her woolen shawl around her shoulders, but before she made it to the door, a timid knock sounded. On the stoop, to her utter dismay, stood Bess - with Jedediah's children.

"Yer father sent us," Bess said. Aggie leaped forward and threw her arms around the woman. The children showed the first emotion Enid had seen, letting out little cries of joy and hugging Aggie fiercely. Over Aggie's head, Bess said, "There be trouble down south, and they's gone to fight. We to stay here until they return."

"Come in," Enid said, masking her surprise with politeness. Until her father and Jedediah returned, she was mistress of the household. She turned to Aggie. "Put the children in my room. I'll stay in Father's, but the linens will need washing. I must go fetch the medicine man for my grandmother now. Please see to her comfort while I'm gone. Try to get her to eat."

Aggie nodded.

It was cold out, bitterly so, but the sky was cloudless. Enid walked briskly, thinking of her grandmother and happier times. No matter how poor they'd been or how miserably her father had treated her, Elizabeth had been a bright spot in this life. Tears trickled out of her eyes and froze on her cheeks.

She skirted the village, following along a row of harvested corn through the Hornsby family's southernmost field and trudging through the wide marshy meadow beyond. There was no path, so she kept an eye out for the landmark that would tell her she was close; a huge, weather-worn grey rock the size of a bus in Sorcha's world. When she spotted the stone jutting up from its otherwise flat surroundings, she noticed as she got closer that cracks in the stone made a vague pattern, like the head of a bear with its mouth open wide.

By the time she reached the medicine man's longhouse, the sun had heated the frigid air somewhat and the exercise had warmed her. From what her grandmother had told her, the longhouse had once been home to many people, but now, as far as Enid knew, the hermit occupied the large structure alone. Two mangy dogs began barking and rushed to within a few feet of her skirt. She froze in the path and stood very still, avoiding eye contact as they snarled at her, kicking up dust in their fury. A shout from within the structure sent the dogs scrabbling away as quickly as they'd arrived. A tall figure exited the longhouse and strode towards her, musket held casually in his left hand. He was dressed in a coarse linen tunic and pants, and his black hair, what little there was of it, stood straight up in a scalp lock on the crown of his shaved head. He was either young enough to have no beard, or clean-shaven. As he got closer, she saw that his nose and ears were pierced with rings of silver. His brown eyes held no welcome.

He looked her up and down and must have mistaken her for a Native American because he said something in his language. Although she had picked up several Mahican words here and there, her father had forbidden Elizabeth from teaching Enid her mother's native tongue. She shook her head and said, "I come to speak with Bear Talker."

He just frowned, so she tried the word for bear, "Machq?"

The young man's frown deepened. "Bear Talker sees no one."

"Please. It's urgent." She cursed the wavering of her voice, trying to keep her emotions at bay.

He shrugged as if he couldn't care less and turned back to the longhouse, leaving her standing there with her mouth hanging open in dismay. A horse whinnied plaintively from somewhere in the trees. She couldn't go back home with her grandmother's last request unfulfilled.

"Tell him..." she said to the young man's retreating back, "...tell him I'm the girl with two spirits."

The young man stopped dead in his tracks. He slowly turned and this time his eyes held wary enquiry. His hand was clenching the musket so tightly she could clearly see the defined muscles in his forearm. It suddenly occurred to her to wonder why a Native American warrior was in her village, especially now that most, if not all of the men had just gone off to war.

"My grandmother Elizabeth is dying."

His scowl came back. With evident contempt, he said, "And you think he can save her."

She shook her head earnestly. "No one can save her. She seeks peace."

He turned away again. "Tell her to seek it from her Christian god."

She bristled at his dismissiveness and his assumption that Elizabeth was Christian, but the animal skin covering the entrance to the longhouse was swept aside by an unseen hand and another voice joined the conversation. The voice was male and authoritative, snapping out curt words Enid didn't understand. The young man called out his answer and after a brief hesitation, the medicine man himself stepped into the light. Enid had seen him from a distance on more than one occasion, but he seemed smaller, shriveled almost, up close.

She stood her ground as the old man approached. He was dressed as plainly as the warrior, but his hair wasn't shaved – he wore it in two braids just like her grandmother, only shorter. He walked with a slight limp and the skin of his face, neck and hands was the color of teak and heavily wrinkled. As he passed the warrior, he gave a quiet order that the young man rushed off to obey.

Bear Talker pointed a shaky finger at her and said, almost accusingly, "You do not have two spirits."

She blinked in confusion but thought it would be impolite to disagree, especially since she needed to convince him to come with her into the village from which he'd been banned long ago. She didn't have to say anything, however, because he wasn't done talking.

"Pohtommauwaus divided your spirit between two bodies," he declared. "Tell me, divided one, what is the name of your other half?"

Enid found she couldn't look away from the intense black eyes blazing out of Bear Talker's raisin face. For fear of being labeled a witch, she'd never discussed her other life with anyone but Elizabeth. Yet he was the one who'd prophesied her condition in the first place, and the force of his personality seemed to coax a response out of her now. Her lips parted and she said quietly, "Sorcha."

"And when does she live?"

Enid caught her breath in a sharp intake. *He really did know.* After a moment, she admitted, "Far in the future."

"I will come with you to ease your grandmother's passing; she is an old friend, but I would ask a boon of you in return. My people were driven

26

from these lands but have tried to live in peace among the other nations. Now the Mohawk encourage us to join the British crown in this fight against the colonials. Who will win this conflict? Which side should my people choose?"

Enid felt as if her heart had dropped into her feet. The warrior was rounding the longhouse, leading two horses in their direction. He'd slung his musket and a leather haversack over his shoulder. She spoke quickly so he wouldn't hear. "There is a thing in Sorcha's world called the butterfly effect. It refers to the theory that if a person were to travel back in time, anything they do could alter the future. Even so small a thing as accidently crushing a butterfly could change the course of history. It has always served as a warning to me to keep my own counsel about what is to come."

Bear Talker held his hand out to the warrior, who halted on the spot, still out of earshot. Enid didn't know if he'd stopped him so the warrior wouldn't overhear the rest of their conversation or whether the medicine man was sending her a subtle warning: answer the question or I won't go.

His smile didn't seem threatening as he responded, "Yet you have lived both of your lives and I will wager you have crushed many an insect in this one. Mayhap nothing you do can change the future because it is already written."

She couldn't fault his logic, and the longer they waited, the more likely it was that Elizabeth would die before they arrived. She made a split-second decision.

"I will not give you details, but I will tell you this: the colonial army will eventually prevail and win their freedom from the crown."

He studied her face. She felt that all her knowledge of the treatment of Native Americans by the United States government over the course of the next 240 years was there for him to see. But he nodded, waved the warrior forward and allowed the younger man to seat him on the smaller of the two saddleless horses.

"This is my brother's youngest son, Joseph," the medicine man said, and kicked his horse into a trot.

Before Enid realized what was happening, Joseph hoisted her up on the other horse as if she were a weightless sack of barley. He mounted behind her with as little effort; it was clear he was an accomplished horseman. As they began traveling back the way she had come, she braced herself for the same uncomfortable sensations she'd experienced riding with Jedediah. Sitting sideways in front of Joseph with her hands tangled tightly in the horse's mane and her torso twisted to face front, it proved impossible to hold herself away from him. Within minutes of trying, she gave up and allowed her hip and back to settle against his body as much as the jostling motion of the trot would allow.

To her surprise, he smelled only faintly of sweat; not the overpowering tang of body odor coming off of Jedediah. His voice in her ear startled her. "What is your name?"

"Enid," she replied. "You speak English very well. Where did you learn?"

"From my parents, same as you." He sounded annoyed. "Your grandmother is Mahican?"

"Yes. My mother as well."

"Is your father English?" She felt him tense a bit as he waited for the answer.

"Irish."

Joseph grunted, and she took it to mean 'same difference.'

They didn't talk after that, because the path evened out and Bear Talker urged his horse into a canter. Joseph followed suit. The children were out front playing when they arrived. They stared as Enid and the two Native American men went into the house. Through the window, she saw Bess and Aggie hanging wet linens on the line out back. The house smelled of cooked cabbage, which meant Bess had probably used the last of the pork in a stew for the mid-day meal.

Enid asked Bear Talker to wait for a moment while she went up to prepare Elizabeth. Her grandmother was sleeping, however, so she came back down and held up one of her homemade surgical masks.

"This will prevent the disease that is killing my grandmother from transferring to you."

Bear Talker's lips puckered in his raisin face. "Is this magic from the future?"

Enid thought about taking the easy way out and saying yes, but the specter of the thousands of Native Americans killed by diseases brought over by Europeans made her say, "No, it is not magic. In the future, many truths are known. One of them is that there are tiny creatures, too small for the eye to see, that travel through the air or water or by touch to make a well man ill. You should never breathe the same air as that of someone dying of disease, and be sure to wash your hands with lye soap after touching them."

The medicine man allowed her to fasten the mask over his nose and mouth. Through the cloth, he said, "Creatures, evil spirits, what is the difference? But I will remember the advice you have given me."

He went up to see Elizabeth then, leaving Enid and Joseph alone in the main room. Joseph looked around, his discomfort evident in the small, nervous movement of his fingers against his thighs.

"You may sit if you like," she offered.

He shrugged a little but sat in a chair by the door and rested the ever-present musket on his knees. He was a very incongruous presence in the little house. She sat across from him and to keep her hands busy as she waited, pulled Elizabeth's needlework, abandoned for some weeks since she took to her bed, into her lap.

"It is true you have two spirits?" Joseph asked after a while.

Enid looked up from tucking and pulling the thread. He wasn't a handsome young man, but when his face wasn't scowling he looked almost approachable. "Your uncle says I have one spirit split in two."

A fleeting smile crossed his lips. In an echo of his uncle's words, he said, "What is the difference? Do they both not live inside you?"

She shook her head but didn't clarify. From upstairs came the sound of low chanting and the repetitive shoosh-shoosh of Bear Talker's rattle. She closed her eyes and prayed that Elizabeth would find peace before her suffering ended. A creak of the floorboards alerted her, and she opened them again.

Bess and Aggie hovered in the doorway from the kitchen. The children were practically hidden in Aggie's skirts; they had probably informed her of Enid's arrival with their unusual guests.

Enid set the needlework aside and rose to her feet, unsure of the proper etiquette. Sorcha would introduce everyone and expect them all to get along as if class wasn't a distinction. Enid was all for that, but the rest of them would find it odd to say the least.

Bess said, "They's a stew on, Miss."

Enid glanced at Joseph, who definitely looked interested. *Ah, to hell with it*, she thought.

"Why don't we all eat, then?" she said.

They had no table in the common room – Enid's father had only ever invited into the house the kind of hard men who ate with their fingers and wiped their hands on their clothes. She'd served them at the small kitchen table as they drank ale and talked of the rebellion, staying well clear of their wandering hands.

There were only four chairs that were soon occupied by Enid and Joseph on one side, and Sarah and Ezekiel, whose chins barely cleared the height of the table, on the other. Bess and Aggie made sure Enid had everything she needed and left to eat their meal on the back porch.

The children ate quietly and with perfect manners, except for the fact that they stared at Joseph with wide, blinking blue eyes the entire time. He ate rapidly, ignoring them. Enid twice attempted to start a conversation, but the children were too shy to even reply, and Joseph only offered monosyllabic responses. It was a very awkward dynamic.

When Bear Talker came into the kitchen, Enid excused herself and took the stairs two at a time, unconcerned that she'd essentially abandoned the children with two strange Native American men.

Elizabeth was asleep; her stringy grey hair spread over the pillow and her breathing as labored and rough as it had been that morning. The room smelled of burnt sage. Whatever the medicine man had accomplished, it wasn't a cure. Enid held her grandmother's limp, arthritic hand, crying softly for an hour or so as memory after happy memory played vividly in her mind. When she ventured back downstairs, Bear Talker and his nephew were gone, and the children and servants waited for their instructions.

Chapter Five

Sorcha

For perhaps the first time since she'd been aware of the differences between her worlds, Sorcha didn't want to be in this one. As soon as she opened her eyes she wanted to go back to Elizabeth. Her last glimpse of Enid's grandmother had been when she left her sleeping fitfully, drugged into unconsciousness by something Bear Talker had left for her. Enid hadn't wanted to frighten Aggie and Bess if they tried and couldn't wake her, so she confessed to them that she was afflicted with a sleeping sickness and that they should respond if Elizabeth needed help in the night. She left them with instructions to keep water in the iron kettle hanging over the fire, and told them how to aid her grandmother should she suffer a fit. Since the children were sleeping in her room, she'd retired to her father's freshly made bed reluctantly, afraid that on the morrow Elizabeth would be gone.

Sorcha took a long, listless shower, trying hard not to cry. For some reason, her fragmented thoughts kept returning to Joseph and how much he reminded her of Ben even though the two were nothing alike physically. Joseph was around the same height, but stockier than Ben, his muscles more compact; and Ben's facial features were more refined, especially the narrow curve of his jaw. Compared to Ben, Joseph was…blunt, was the most accurate word that came to mind – like comparing a hammer to a knife. The only thing the two young men had in common was their Native American ancestry.

As she dressed in loose-fitting jeans and three lightweight layered t-shirts, she knew it would be impossible to push Enid's world behind her usual barrier. She had a big history test she hadn't studied for but couldn't muster up the slightest bit of concern over the dismal grade she was about to get.

Overnight a stiff wind had stripped most of the leaves from the old oak. The sky was heavy with dark rain clouds, a fitting atmosphere for her mood.

Paula greeted her cheerfully with, "Hey, no Loony today," and it took Sorcha a moment to realize she meant Luanne.

She got into the car and removed her history book from her backpack. They were studying the Civil War; a time period Sorcha was only marginally familiar with. Paula glanced over at her and said, "You okay?"

Sorcha thought about telling her about Elizabeth but figured Paula's sympathy would break the fragile dam holding back her tears. "Fine. You ready for the test?"

It was the only class they had together. Paula chuckled and said, "No. You?"

"I might get a 'D' if I'm lucky."

A few fat raindrops hit the windshield, so Paula switched on the wipers. Within seconds the drops changed to hail that bounced off the car. Paula was forced to slow down as the hail began coming down heavily, significantly reducing visibility. By the time they got to the school's overflow parking lot, the downpour had stopped.

Sorcha was glad she was wearing her faux-fur lined windbreaker and waterproof boots as she forced the car door open against the wind and stepped out into a slushy mud puddle. She and Paula walked a meandering path across the field to avoid more puddles. Paula was watching the ground, so she didn't see what happened, but Sorcha did.

On the paved parking lot up ahead, Ben rode his bike past Paula's crush, Dalton Boyle, and three of his friends. She saw Ben swerve close to the group in order to go around a huge puddle, but his tire hit the edge of the puddle anyway and sent a fine spray up onto the lower half of Dalton's jeans. Dalton looked down at his pants and sneered in disgust, his teeth flashing white in his dark-skinned face. He shouted an obscenity after Ben, who stopped to look back – only to get a face full of the slushy-snowball Dalton had hastily scooped together from the back of a nearby car. Ben got off the bike and thrust it angrily to the pavement.

"Oh, no," Sorcha murmured.

Paula looked up and asked, "What?" But the scene spoke for itself as Ben stalked over to within about a foot of Dalton, who stood his ground, flanked by his friends. Sorcha wanted to look away but couldn't. The young men exchanged angry words, most of which Sorcha couldn't make out since they were blown away on the wind. As she and Paula got closer, Ben looked over at her. She shook her head faintly, pleading with her eyes for him to back down.

To her surprise, he did, taking a step back and relaxing his clenched fists. She clearly heard him say, "It was an accident, man." Dalton didn't look appeased; in fact, he seemed to become more confident of his superior advantage. His arm shot out and he thumped Ben in the shoulder with the heel of his hand.

Before Ben could respond, Paula astonished everyone present by screaming, "Dalton Boyle, you leave him alone!"

The words were quite possibly the first Paula had spoken to Dalton in years. He turned to her, anger and disbelief on his face. "Mind your own damned business!"

Paula had two flaming patches of red on her cheeks and her eyes were dark with fury. "It's everyone's business when it's four against one! Man up, Dalton." She spit his name out with all the contempt four years of being ignored by a guy can produce.

Dalton looked as if she'd slapped him. His jaw was clenched tightly as he glared at Ben and back again to Paula. "Yeah, whatever," he snapped.

He began walking away but made sure to bump Ben roughly with his shoulder as he went past. His friends were less subtle: one boy pointed a finger in Ben's face and said, "Watch yourself." Another said, "Next time your little girlfriend won't be around to protect you, Webster."

If Paula thought Ben was going to stick around and thank her, she was mistaken. He merely tossed Sorcha a look she couldn't decipher before picking his bike up and riding off. Paula did exactly what Sorcha expected her to do: burst into tears. Sorcha put her arm around Paula's shoulders and steered her away from the prying eyes of random students attracted to the disturbance. They ended up back in Paula's car, where they stayed until Paula got control of herself and had fixed her runny make-up.

Sorcha was late for first period but didn't particularly care. As soon as she sat in her seat, her thoughts flew back to Elizabeth. Later, when she went to her locker to get her sack lunch, there was a note from Paula.

"Sorry, Sorch, but I'm going home sick and you'll need to find another ride. Talk to you later. P."

Paula's 'sickness' probably involved her heart more than anything. Sorcha wished she could smack Dalton for sending her friend's self-esteem into another tailspin.

Sorcha's parents, Michael and Amelia, commuted into the city together for their respective jobs, almost a hundred miles one way, so not only did she rarely see them, but she couldn't count on them for a ride. She called her grandmother and left a message, but it was Wednesday, the one day of the week Fay wasn't home – she spent each Wednesday pitching in at a homeless shelter in Poughkeepsie.

33

By the end of the school day when Fay hadn't returned her call, she resigned herself to taking the bus, but then she went and took too long trudging to the bus stop and missed it. The schedule mounted under plastic on the inside of the dirty, graffiti-defaced bench shelter told her the next bus would be an hour coming. If she walked, she'd be halfway home by then, so she zipped her jacket, tightened the strings of the hood against the wind and set off.

If she thought the unaccustomed exercise would take her mind off Elizabeth, she was mistaken. The wind blew the clouds across the sky, reminding her of one of Enid's favorite childhood games. She and Elizabeth would sit in the grass, weaving baskets and watching the clouds, calling out when they saw a recognizable shape: "Look, there's an eagle. A bunny! A mushroom!" Then Elizabeth would tell a story about all the shapes they'd seen, but said it was really the Cloud People who were telling it; they sent the shapes as a message to anyone below who could interpret it.

Today she saw a whale, a hook-nosed man's profile and a coffin.

She made it out of town and had almost reached the dirt path that paralleled the highway when the driver of a truck ahead of her performed a screeching half-donut in the street, sending up stinking puffs of burnt rubber and leaving black tire marks on the road. She could see there were four occupants, but the truck shot past so fast she couldn't make out any of their faces.

"Wow, impressive," she said to nobody, shaking her head. She'd seen the jacked-up truck before, parked at school. Whoever was driving was either in some kind of major hurry, was immaturely showing off for his friends, or both.

She crossed the street and ducked through the tear in the chain-link fence that had been erected to keep pedestrians off the privately-owned land all along one side of the highway. The landowner had long ago stopped mending the fence, probably because it had become a losing battle. The popular path was several feet wide with well-packed dirt. Sorcha had walked it many times, but never alone.

The first thing she saw was a bicycle lying on its side in a patch of wild grass. Right away she recognized it as Ben's. She looked around for him, doubting he was just sitting somewhere taking a break. The ground showed multiple deep footprints, many with long streaks plowing through the mud, evidence of a violent scuffle. The driver of the truck hadn't been showing off; he'd been beating a hasty retreat from the scene of a crime. Sure enough, she saw a prone body several yards off the path, almost hidden in the wild grass.

She ran, slipping in the mud and falling to her knees next to him. Grasping his shoulder, she heaved him onto his side; terrified by what she would find when she saw his face. Ben groaned and tried to elbow her away, but she said, "Knock it off, I'm trying to help you."

He struggled to a sitting position and muttered, "I'm fine. Go away."

She ignored him, taking stock of his injuries. His left eye was swollen, and he had a fat, bloody lip, but otherwise it seemed as if the worst of it was the knuckles on his right hand, which looked as if he'd pulverized them against a wall. She took his hand and he gasped and snatched it away.

"You need to see a doctor," she said.

He scoffed. "Yeah, that's gonna happen. What the hell are you doing here?"

She ignored the question. "Were you unconscious at all? We should call the police."

His uninjured hand shot out and stopped her from reaching around to her backpack. "I was just taking a nap. No doctor, no cops, nothing – understand?"

He got to his feet and staggered to his bike. Sorcha stood and watched as he straddled it and fit his foot to the pedal. A drop of rain hit her cheek.

She fully expected him to ride off and leave her, but he said, "You shouldn't be out here alone."

She walked over to him. He'd just gotten jumped and beat up and was worried about her.

"Should I be watching out for your homeless relatives here, too?"

He laughed and immediately winced. With his good hand, he gently probed his lip. "Do I look bad?"

Her eyes dropped to his feet and back. "You mean the face or the mud?"

He smiled, winced again and requested, "No jokes, okay?"

She made a cross-your-heart motion as he got back off his bike and began pushing it.

She walked next to him. "Where's your backpack?"

"Bastards took it."

"Was it Dalton's buddies? And don't lie, because I recognized the truck from school, and it'd be easy to figure out who drives it."

"It wasn't them," was all he said. It was sprinkling now. "How far to your house?"

"It's a ways."

"I've never seen you walk before."

She sighed. "Paula's never bailed on me before."

35

He glanced over. "She kinda went nuts this morning. She and that Dalton kid have history?"

Sorcha had no idea why she said it, but the words, "Only in her fantasy world," slipped off her tongue. She was instantly appalled that she'd given away her best friend's deepest secret, and revealed it to a virtual stranger, no less. A young man who'd spent the last two years in juvenile hall – and quite possibly the last person she should trust.

He didn't respond; just gave her an inscrutable sidelong look. Stunned by her betrayal, she walked woodenly next to him as the occasional car whizzed by on the highway.

The rain began in earnest and after about ten minutes of slogging through it, her pant legs were soaked. With no warning, Ben cut across her path and said, "Come on."

He led her away from the highway down a barely discernible path to a copse of pine trees planted in a rough circle. Someone had trimmed the lowest branches to several feet above her head. The afternoon clouds made the day dark and it was darker still under the trees, but they provided perfect cover from the downpour; only a stray drop or two reached them. Ben leaned his bike against one of the trees and kicked the thick layer of ground cover away from the base of another. When he'd cleared a good patch, he sat down, rested his forearms casually on his knees, and looked at her expectantly. Even with the black eye and fat lip; even covered head to toe in mud – he was gorgeous. His casual assumption that she would sit next to him made her heart skip a beat.

Suddenly, there wasn't enough air under the trees and her feet felt firmly planted to the spot. To stall, she fumbled with the ties of her hood and pushed it off her hair. Before he noticed her reluctance, she blurted out the first thing that came to mind. "How did you know about this place?"

"Used to be holy ground for my people many moons ago." He said it sarcastically, but she suspected he meant it. She looked around and something about the area seemed not just familiar, but that annoying déjà vu kind of familiar that had been plaguing her lately. Beyond the far outer trees, a huge rock loomed. She stared at it for several seconds. Could it be? With a hop in her step, she cut through the trees and worked her way around until she could see the other side of the rock face. The natural monument was invisible from the highway, which is why she'd never seen it in Sorcha's world, but this was definitely the rock near the medicine man's longhouse. It was a strange coincidence that she'd just been here, 'yesterday,' Enid's time.

"Bear Talker. The longhouse." She didn't realize she'd said it out loud until her arm was grabbed from behind and Ben pulled her around to face him.

"What did you say?"

His vehemence startled her. "Nothing."

"You said 'Bear Talker.' How did you know about this place?"

She lifted her shoulders defensively. "What's the big deal? It's not a secret, is it?"

His brows came together in a scowl that reminded her of Joseph. "As a matter of fact, it is."

"You're hurting my arm." He wasn't really; she said it to distract him.

He loosened his grip but didn't let go. His face was only inches from hers. She struggled to keep her eyes from dropping to his lips.

Quietly, almost menacingly, he asked, "What do you know about Bear Talker?"

She realized Enid knew almost nothing about the medicine man himself.

"I don't know anything," she said. "Why are you being so weird?"

That seemed to shake him from his determination to find out what she knew. He stepped back and let go of her arm. "I shouldn't have brought you here."

Her cell phone jingled from her backpack. She tossed Ben a wary look and began walking back to the trees as she dug for the phone.

As soon as she answered, Grammy Fay asked, "Where are you?"

"Walking," Sorcha replied.

"In this rain?"

Ben brushed past her and she watched his back disappear under the branches.

"Yeah," she said. "Can you come get me?"

Instead of following Ben and going back into the clearing where Bear Talker's longhouse used to be, she walked around the trees.

"Where are you?" Fay asked.

"On the path along the highway, about halfway." She'd almost reached the path and saw that Ben had gotten his bike and was waiting for her.

"I'll be there as soon as I can."

Sorcha glanced over at Ben's stiff face and thought, *it can't be soon enough*.

Chapter Six

Enid

When she opened her eyes, the first thing Enid saw was Aggie sitting watch in the chair next to her father's bed.

"Has she gone?" Enid asked.

"Yes, Miss," Aggie replied softly. There was sympathy in the slave girl's face, but also stoicism. It would be a long day, starting with preparing the body for burial. Aggie would have experience there with the passing of Jedediah's wife, and for that Enid was grateful. She didn't know how she would get through the day without help. Her father, as mean-spirited as he was, would have taken care of the necessary chores – but he was gone, and it was up to Enid to sew a shroud or procure a coffin, and obtain the headstone and gravediggers.

Enid dressed in a grey dress with black stockings. The dress was very worn and a bit too big since it was Elizabeth's. It had once belonged to a fine lady but had somehow come into her grandmother's possession.

It was cowardly, perhaps, but she found herself unable to go in to look at Elizabeth's body. She didn't want to see her grandmother shriveled and cold; she wanted to remember her full of life and happiness.

The day passed in a blur. The village, normally bustling with activity, seemed deserted since every last man and youth old enough to fire a rifle had been recruited by the militia. The old stonecutter charged by the letter, which solved the mystery of Elizabeth's headstone for her. After using most of the money she'd managed to squirrel away from her father to pay for the plain pine coffin and the gravediggers' time, she had only enough left to purchase an unadorned headstone with a few carefully chosen words. She already knew what those words were, since Sorcha had pondered their meaning for years, wondering why there was no date of death. Enid wouldn't dream of attempting to change the future just to satisfy Sorcha's curiosity.

Enid had no money to purchase black gloves, which were traditionally delivered to the homes of people invited to a funeral. There was no funeral, although the pastor came and solemnly read from the Bible while Bess and Aggie sang. Their voices harmonized perfectly, rising and falling in tandem, echoing out over the field Enid had chosen – the same field that by Sorcha's time would be full of her ancestors.

"And God shall wipe away all tears from their eyes; and there shall be no more death, neither sorrow, nor crying, neither shall there be any more pain: for the former things are passed away," said the pastor.

Enid wondered what words Bear Talker had offered as her grandmother's last rites and prayed that she'd taken comfort from them.

The gravediggers lowered Elizabeth into the ground and covered the coffin with dirt. It would be a few weeks before the gravestone was ready, but the rest had been dealt with swiftly and efficiently.

Enid stayed by the graveside until the sun colored the western sky with streaks of orange and pink. She knelt to set a bouquet of goldenrod on the mound of earth and the tears she'd held in check all day burst forth.

Chapter Seven

Sorcha

Sorcha's first thought upon waking was, *Why me*?

It was a selfish thought, but she couldn't help it. Instead of getting up to take her shower and dress for the day, she lay in bed with the covers over her head as tears leaked out onto her pillow.

Grammy Fay poked her head in after a while and asked, "Are you still in bed? What's the matter?"

When Sorcha pulled the covers down, revealing her tear-stained face, Fay let out a little cry of distress and rushed to sit on the bed to take Sorcha into her arms. They stayed like that for some time, Fay rocking her back and forth and murmuring soothing sounds.

"I'm here, Sweetling. I'm here," Fay said.

"But for how long?" Sorcha cried.

Fay pulled away, grasped her chin and said firmly, "Death is hard. It comes for us all and doesn't always give advance warning. You've known for some time that Elizabeth's illness was terminal, and you've had the luxury of preparing for it. She is no longer suffering. Now it's time to reach down inside of you to find peace. She wouldn't want you to mourn...not like this."

Sorcha knew it was true. Elizabeth had said so herself. She sniffed, and Fay reached out to pull a few tissues from the box by her bed.

"I do, however," Fay said, "think you should stay home today. We'll tell the school you're sick, okay?"

Sorcha nodded, glad she wouldn't have to put on a brave face today of all days. While Fay called and made her excuses to the school secretary, Sorcha texted Paula to tell her she wouldn't need a ride.

Almost immediately, her cell rang. Paula said, "I'm sorry I left you in the lurch yesterday. You don't need to ride in with your grandmother – I'll pick you up."

"It's not that," Sorcha replied. "Elizabeth died and I'm not up to going to school today."

"Oh, my God, I'm so sorry! Oh, Sorch…how awful. I know you haven't wanted to talk about it, but I'm here for you whenever you do."

"Thanks…same thing goes for you – you know, with Dalton."

Paula let out a short laugh. "There is no Dalton and never has been. I'm over it, I swear."

Sorcha secretly thought it was easier said than done, but responded, "Good. He doesn't deserve you."

"He's irrelevant. What's important are friendships that really exist. I wish I could do something to make you feel better."

"Time heals all wounds." Sorcha tried to say it with conviction. "And Elizabeth died two hundred and thirty-six years ago."

"Too bad to you it feels like yesterday."

It was *yesterday*, Sorcha thought. Paula's empathy was real, but the way she expressed it, the actual wording she used, hinted that no matter how often Paula assured her she believed Enid existed – she didn't – at least not unequivocally. But that wasn't fair to Paula and she knew it. Her friend had been nothing but loyal and look what she'd done: blabbing to Ben yesterday about Paula's crush on Dalton.

Paula said, "Hey, I gotta go, but you want me to come over after school?"

"No, that's okay. I think Grammy Fay has plans for me today."

They rang off, and Sorcha soon discovered that Fay did, indeed, have plans for her. The morning had dawned warm and mild, in stark contrast to the storm that had blown through the day before. After feeding Sorcha a hearty breakfast that Sorcha did her best to eat, Fay dragged her out to the garden greenhouse, a dainty cedar wood and glass structure built against the side of the house. She handed Sorcha a pair of gloves and some snippers and gestured to her prized container rose bushes.

"I think these would look better gracing Elizabeth's headstone, don't you?" she asked.

Chapter Eight

Enid

She put the grey dress and black hose on again and walked out to the lone mound of fresh earth as the sun made its appearance in the eastern sky. She felt encapsulated in a bubble of grief that kept the beauty of the sunrise from touching her, but there was too much to do today to dwell on her sadness.

Chores they'd fallen behind on needed attending to, particularly the harvesting of the last of the late apples from the seven trees in her father's little orchard. Enid enlisted the aid of Sarah and Ezekiel, who picked up the fallen fruit and sorted the rotten ones out to give to the hogs, while she, Aggie and Bess plucked what remained from the branches. Once the apples were stored in the root cellar, they took their mid-day meal.

Enid ate in the kitchen with the children, again attempting to engage them in conversation and again failing to get much out of them.

"Do you know how to read and write?" she asked.

Ezekiel, with his hair a shade or two blonder than his sister after a summer in the sun, shook his head no.

"Do you know your alphabet?" she asked.

Sarah, the eldest by one year, dutifully recited the letters up to 'J,' but couldn't recall the rest. Enid was not surprised. The poorer the household, the less likely the children could be spared from chores to attend school. Not that the village schoolhouse was any great shakes unless you wanted your catechism pounded into you. Enid had gone sporadically, but in the areas of reading, writing and arithmetic she'd relied solely on Sorcha's education. Thus far, very few of the things Enid had learned to simply survive on a farm in the eighteenth century had been of use in Sorcha's world.

One of those things was making tallow candles, another chore that had been neglected until the last candle in the house had burnt down to a stub, but one in which the children would be of no help. Enid went up to her room and rummaged through her chest until she found some of her old toys, which she gave to the children to play with in the main room. Sarah's eyes went wide when she saw the baby doll Elizabeth had made out of scraps from her needlework.

"Go on, take it," Enid urged. Ezekiel had no such compunctions taking the wooden top and blocks she handed him.

While the fat rendered in a big pot on the fire, Enid baked bread, and the sound of the children playing in the next room brought a smile to her lips for the first time in days.

The more distasteful and strenuous chores her father usually attended to fell to Bess and Aggie: she'd sent them to the west field to muck out the pigpen. The kitchen window was wide open in order to air out the overpowering smell of rendered fat. Enid looked outside, surprised to see a thick column of smoke rising from where the village was situated. It was no ordinary bonfire; that was clear from the size of it. A building must have caught fire. She rushed into the main room and hushed the children so she could listen. Faint pops and booms echoed through the chill afternoon air. Gunfire – and too much of it to attribute to someone out hunting in the area.

Frightened, she said, "Children, get your coat and shawl, quickly!"

She went back into the kitchen and taking the bucket of water from the corner, put out the fires in the hearth and the oven, filling the room with steam. She fanned the air with her apron until it cleared. After closing the window, she shoved the still warm loaves of bread into a sack and slipped a small knife into her pocket. Looking around, she hoped it wouldn't be obvious to anyone who came into the house that the occupants had recently left. She picked Ezekiel up and set him against her hip; he obligingly clung to her, his thin body weighing nearly nothing. She shooed Sarah out the front door and then grabbed her hand and ran, practically dragging the little girl along with her, to the west field.

Aggie and Bess had finished with the pigpen and were on their way back to the house. Enid didn't have to say a word; they'd seen the smoke and heard the gunfire and knew what it probably meant. Bess lifted Sarah into her arms, and they all hurried towards the woods.

When Enid was twelve years old, her father brought her out here to a stand of mature trees. It was not long after the village had gotten news of what would one day be called The Boston Massacre.

"See this tree?" he'd asked. It was a stout oak near the middle of the grove.

"Yes, father."

"Here be a good place ta hide should anyone come round the house ye'd need ta get away from, ye ken?"

She looked up, thinking he meant her to climb it and hide among the branches, but he walked around to the far side of the trunk, revealing a deep black hollow.

"It smells like a skunk den," Enid said.

"Aye, it were. But I kilt the critters and plan to fix a door here so's no one can tell it's not part o' the tree."

Her father may not have been tender and caring, but he loved her in his way, and his solution to the practical matter of where to go should the enemy come knocking was inspired.

Enid wrestled with the door her father had fashioned from an old log. The iron hinges had rusted from years of being out in the elements, but it finally opened on the cobwebby darkness within. She hustled the children and servants into the crevasse, but Bess' bulk took too much space and there wasn't enough room for Enid.

"No, Miss, I's the one should stay outside," Bess said, but Enid would have none of it.

"Don't fret, I'll be fine. Stay hidden until I come for you." She handed Aggie the sack of bread. "With luck they won't come past the house anyway."

Once she'd shut the door on them, she knelt to brush her hand over the dirt to obliterate their footsteps. For good measure, she gathered an armful of fallen leaves and scattered it over the dirt.

She decided to head for the creek, which would take her past the back of the house. There were thick thorn bushes growing there, with enough room for her to hide within, but still be able to see the house and the tree where the children and servants were hiding.

A drumming sound, like rolling thunder, alerted her to approaching horsemen. She hiked up her skirts and bolted from the relative safety of the oak grove. If she were caught, she didn't want to be anywhere near the others.

Moments before the house blocked her view, she glimpsed a band of about five or six men on horseback, galloping up the trail from the village. They were too far away for her to see them well and she prayed they hadn't seen her at all. She doubted she would make it to the creek but had no choice but to try. She'd just put on an extra burst of speed when a figure in her peripheral vision appeared out of nowhere and grabbed her. A hand muffled her startled scream as her accoster used her momentum to lift her bodily and swing her around. She struggled as he carried her several yards away. Before she knew it, she was lying prone in the grass underneath him.

Terrified, she fought him, trying to think of the moves Sorcha had learned in self-defense class, but he grunted, "Lie still!" and she recognized Joseph's voice. She froze in surprise, only her chest moving up and down as she attempted to catch her breath, which wasn't easy with his hand over her mouth. He stared into her eyes and must have been satisfied that she would no longer fight him because he slowly lowered his hand and pulled his arm out from under her.

She ignored her first impulse to ask him why he was here. His actions had already demonstrated he was there to protect her, although she couldn't fathom why. "Who are they?" she whispered.

"Mohawk," he replied.

"War party?"

"No. They travel to New York to escort their chief north."

She didn't ask what happened in the village. Bear Talker's words from two days ago came back to her: "Now the Mohawk encourage us to join the British crown in this fight against the colonials." The horsemen would have considered it good fortune to happen upon an undefended patriot village where they could help themselves to anything they desired – all in the name of the crown.

He shifted himself off her, staying low to the ground. With his upper body resting on his elbows, he reached out and produced his musket. She rolled over and saw that he'd dragged her behind a slight crest in the field that offered natural cover. They watched the house through the tall grass; there was nothing to see, but plenty to hear. From the crashing and banging it was clear the Mohawk warriors were inside. There hadn't been time for the pot of fat to cool. They would know the occupants had just left.

After a few minutes, two of them came out. One walked cautiously toward the creek and the other went in the direction of the west field.

"The children…" Enid whispered urgently. She started to crawl backward in the grass, but he stopped her.

"It will not help if you are caught."

"What are they looking for?"

"I guess they already found it – shelter for the night."

"No, I mean those two," she said, nodding to the men slowly walking the perimeter.

He gave a slight shrug as if it were obvious. "You."

She closed her eyes and shivered. Of course the Mohawk would want to make sure the occupants of the house they planned to squat in weren't nearby – or a threat. The one who'd gone toward the west field circled back without finding the hollow tree. The other one looked inside the barn and the chicken coop and also came back around to the house. It was

45

getting dark and the temperature had dropped. One of them went into the house, but to her dismay, the other sat in her father's chair on the back porch and lit what was quite possibly her father's pipe.

Joseph said, "We will wait until Grandmother Moon is high -"

"I cannot."

He looked at her inquiringly.

"I will fall asleep by then. The spirit in this body cannot be woken while the spirit in my other body is awake."

She'd confirmed that she had two lives, and he must have had no trouble believing it because her revelation didn't faze him. "Must you sleep?"

"I'm afraid it cannot be helped."

He frowned and squinted at the house. "Have you ale?"

"Yes."

"Good."

The hours passed slowly. As Joseph predicted, the men in her house found her father's ale, and if the noise and laughter echoing out over the field was any indication, drank a good quantity of it. Enid had begun to shake uncontrollably from the cold, so Joseph pulled her impersonally into his arms. He was dressed less warmly than she, but the heat emanating off his body astonished her. She threw modesty to the wind and snuggled up against him. He kept a close eye on the house, but every few minutes checked to make sure she was still awake.

The last thing she remembered was the feel of his rough shirt against her cheek and the sound of his slow, steady heartbeat.

Chapter Nine

Sorcha

She sat up abruptly in bed and cried, "No-no-no-no-no!" Enid couldn't have fallen asleep at a worse time. Sorcha grabbed her pillow and buried her face in it, swearing profusely into its softness.

Her door burst open and Grammy Fay rushed in. "Are you alright?"

Sorcha dropped the pillow and responded in a plaintive whine, "*I'm fine. Not so sure about Enid, though.*" She filled Fay in on the events at the farm; her words pouring forth with her emotion.

Fay sank down onto the side of the bed with a heavy sigh, patting Sorcha on the leg. "There's nothing you can do about it, so I suggest you pull yourself together, Sweetling."

"I wish I could go back." It was the first time Sorcha had ever uttered that sentiment. She gave Fay a hopeful look and said, "Maybe if I take a sleeping pill...?"

Fay pursed her lips disapprovingly. "None of the medications your doctors gave you as a child made any difference," she reminded her. "You said you thought Enid could trust this Joseph fellow, right?"

Sorcha dropped her head in her hands and rubbed the sleep out of her eyes with her index fingers. She saw Joseph's fierce face and kind eyes. "I suppose."

"And he said the Mohawk are just passing through, so I'll bet when you go back it'll all be over, and everything will be fine."

Sorcha had her doubts, but as Fay had pointed out, there was nothing she could do. She got out of bed and into the shower, trying to downshift from the excitement of Enid's world to her mundane existence in this one.

The rest of the day started out just as ordinarily as any other, except the ride to school with Paula was like picking a scab off a fresh wound. Paula coaxed her into talking about Elizabeth, and as much as she'd rather push the painful feelings aside, at least she didn't have to explain about Joseph and the Mohawk and Enid falling asleep in the midst of it all.

After History class, Mr. Lee made her stay after to discuss the 'D' she'd gotten on her test.

"The first month in class you were averaging an 'A,' Miss Sloane. What's going on with you?" he asked.

The first month of class they'd studied the Revolutionary War. She was briefly tempted to tell him her grandmother died but squelched the urge. She couldn't very well back it up if he were to contact her parents, and besides, it seemed disloyal to Elizabeth to use her sadness as an excuse, even though it was true.

"I'll try harder," she said.

Mr. Lee offered to give her extra credit to make up the 'D' and she took it, mostly to get him off her case. She wanted to care about her History grade, but in the big scheme of things, it just didn't rate very highly.

By noon, she was on edge to the point of being twitchy. She and Paula ate their respective lunches as the minute hand of the clock taunted her with its slowness. Ben was conspicuous by his absence from the lunchroom. She wondered if he'd come to school at all the last two days. He'd taken quite a beating, but from the look of his knuckles, had given as good as he got. She studied the faces around the room but didn't see anyone who looked like they'd been at the other end of those knuckles.

In place of fifth period, they had to sit through a pep rally for the football team. She and Paula had attended every game for the last three years so Paula could secretly cheer on Dalton, who was a rather indifferent linebacker. There was a rare Saturday game tomorrow.

"Are we going?" Sorcha asked.

Paula's shoulders drooped. "Probably shouldn't, huh?"

"You still like him."

"Of course I do."

Sorcha patted her on the back. "Then we're going."

After school, on the way to Paula's car, she made a point of sauntering past the truck she'd seen peeling out just before she'd found Ben face-down in the grass. It was jacked up too high for her to see into the side window. Casually, she asked Paula, "Whose truck is this?"

"Um, you know Terri Frazier's ex-boyfriend? I forget his name, but he's a senior."

"John Nelson, isn't it? Wasn't he the guy Ben beat up and got put in juvie for?" Things were starting to make sense now. Ben had gotten jumped as payback.

They reached Paula's car. "Yeah, but I heard it didn't happen like that." Paula was talking to Sorcha over the hood, but she stopped, and her gaze shifted. Sorcha turned just as Ben rode up next to her on his bike.

He said, "Can I talk to you?"

"What happened to your face?" Paula asked.

His jaw tightened and he lifted his eyebrows at Sorcha.

"Sure," she said, and followed him to a patch of trampled grass too far away for Paula to hear.

"I'm sorry I was a jerk the other day." He appeared to be inspecting the ground when he said it, but he sounded sincere.

"It's alright."

He looked at her then. "It's not alright. You helped me when a lot people would have left 'that scumbag juvenile delinquent' to rot out there."

She tilted her head. "I think it'd take a lot more than John Nelson and his friends to keep you down."

She watched, fascinated, as he fought the smile that crept over his lips and lost. With a little laugh, he shook his head. "I got my black belt when I was twelve. John upped his game – he got some moves he didn't have two years ago – but, yeah, it took all four of them to put me in the dirt."

"Mud."

He full-on grinned at that and she caught her breath. His teeth were straight and white, and a dimple winked into existence in his left cheek. It occurred to her suddenly that he'd done a one-eighty from the surly young man she'd walked with in the rain. Was there a reason he seemed to be pouring on the charm?

"What did you want to talk to me about?"

His grin melted away. "It's just…I gotta know…who'd you hear about Bear Talker from?"

She'd had a feeling he was going to ask her that. He'd been so upset about it.

"You tell me why it's so important," she said, "and I'll tell you what I know." She had no intention of telling him the truth but was confident it wouldn't come to that anyway. He'd already said it was a secret; he wasn't going to tell her anything.

But he surprised her with, "Deal. You go first."

"No. You."

His lips thinned in a quick flare of annoyance, but he kept his voice steady. As if he was talking to a three-year-old he said, "If I tell you, there's a very good chance you won't believe me."

That got her attention. Before she stopped to consider the potential ramifications, she heard herself say, "Ditto."

It must have dawned on him that they were at an impasse. "Fine."

"Fine." She started to turn away.

"Wait." He put a hand on her arm and let out a little growl of reluctance. "Okay." He pinched the bridge of his nose between his fingers and said, "I can't believe I'm doing this," before looking intently into her face. "You can't say anything – to anyone."

"I'm good at keeping secrets."

He glanced over at Paula, but she'd gotten into her car and appeared to be reading something. There was no danger of her overhearing, so he seemed to relax somewhat. His next words tumbled out. "I'm only telling you because it's obvious you already know something. So, yeah, I'm part of a – secret society of sorts. We meet there twice a year. There. Now you go. Who told you about Bear Talker?"

A secret society? She almost laughed. It seemed like such a lame reason for him to get so riled up, but obviously he took it pretty seriously. Maybe he thought one of the other members had broken the sacred vow of silence or something and told her about this Bear Talker. She decided to tell a modified version of the truth after all, since she was a bad liar and he had no way of verifying it anyway.

"Bear Talker is a medicine man. He came to help my grandmother Elizabeth cross over into the spirit world. She died yesterday."

He frowned. "Your grandmother's name is Elizabeth? And you *met* Bear Talker. Are you messing with me?"

"Yes, her name was Elizabeth, and I'm all torn up about it, thanks for asking. I can tell you one thing for sure: we're not talking about the same Bear Talker."

"Oh, really? In the woods, you said, 'Bear Talker's longhouse.' If we're not talking about the same guy, what did you mean?"

He had her there. "I – I was talking about someone from the past."

He looked absolutely aghast. In a dark voice, he demanded, "Who told you to say that?"

"No one!" She was getting frustrated with the conversation, and Ben's strangeness was freaking her out. "Why would someone tell me to say it?"

His head went back and forth in almost undetectable little shakes. "No. It's impossible."

She stared back at him, a jolt of panic running through her. He was looking at her as if he'd seen a ghost. This secret society business was serious to him, deadly serious apparently. She reviewed her exact words and

50

couldn't figure out what had him so spooked. He backed away, watching her the entire time, before getting on his bike and riding off.

"What just happened?" she murmured.

She was standing there feeling like something momentous and very, very bad had just occurred when a loud honk startled her. She looked over at Paula, who had her thumbs in the air and a happy, questioning look on her face.

Back in the car, Paula let out a little squeal and said, "Oh, my God, he totally likes you."

Sorcha sighed. "Oh, I doubt there's any danger of that."

"Well, then what was that all about?"

She debated not telling her, but it would take nearly as much effort to brush Paula off as it would to just tell her. So on the ride home, she did.

Chapter Ten

Enid

Not once in her entire life had Enid woken up anywhere but in her bed. When Sorcha had laid down to sleep, she'd hoped that was where Enid would wake up this time, too, but she'd been prepared to find herself out in the open, still in the grass with Joseph.

She was assaulted by confusing sensations when she came to: the sharp smell of horse, the dull sound of hoofs clumping in the dirt, bright light. She was not lying in her soft bed under her warm bedcovers; instead of the comfort and safety of home, she appeared to be draped over the front of a horse.

Once she realized where she was, she assumed Joseph had carried her unconscious body to his mount and was taking her to safety. Her next thought was for the children and servants. She tried to move, but her arms appeared to be bound behind her back. Had he done it to keep them from flopping around? She turned her head to let him know she was awake, but from her head-down position, all she could see of him was his leg.

She focused past the leg to determine where she was, and that's when she saw him. Joseph was not sitting astride the horse. He was face up on the ground in front of her house, eyes closed, arms and legs splayed and tied to stakes driven into the soil. His shirt was missing, and rivulets of dried blood laced his face.

Horrified, Enid struggled against her bonds. Fingers slid into her hair and grasped a handful. The rider lifted her head by her hair, forcing her face towards him. She'd never seen him before, but there was no doubt this man was one of the Mohawk warriors. He said something to her in his language then spat on the ground in Joseph's general direction and laughed.

She didn't speak, just glared her hatred at him. If the quizzical smile he gave her was any indication, he wasn't fazed by her defiance. She held off on her tears until the warrior released her hair and her head dropped back down against his mount's side. He kicked the horse into a walk down the dusty dirt path. She watched Joseph shrink into the distance, praying he was alive. Had the children escaped, or remained hidden? She wondered if she would ever know.

One thing appeared certain: she wouldn't be marrying Jedediah after all.

Hours passed. Her hands had long since gone numb from her bindings and her upper back and neck muscles were knotted into spasms from her attempts to lift her head, which felt like it was going to burst from the blood pooling there. She was thirsty and hungry and desperate to relieve herself. If they didn't stop soon, she was afraid she'd be forced to humiliate herself right there on the horse.

She tried to distract herself from the pain and discomfort, but time takes on new meaning when you're hanging upside down on a hostile Native American's horse. Joseph had said they weren't a war party. If he was still alive, he was probably reevaluating that assumption. He'd said they were headed south to rendezvous with their chief in New York. How had he known? It was logical to assume the party had stopped by Bear Talker's longhouse on the way into the village. She'd looked out the kitchen window and seen that great cloud of smoke. Perhaps it hadn't been coming from the village, but from just outside it – from Bear Talker's longhouse. If the Mohawk had attacked Bear Talker, it might explain why Joseph had come for her. Had the medicine man revealed to them that she could predict the future? Joseph had flat-out said the warriors were looking for her, but she'd given his statement the more generalized meaning that they would be looking for anyone who lived in the house they'd chosen to squat in.

God, her head hurt. She'd compounded it by crying uncontrollably for the first hour, so her eyes were swollen and her sinuses thickly congested. Dust kicked up by the horses ahead of them made it even more difficult to breathe.

The sun was past the mid-day point when they finally stopped. Her captor pulled her roughly from his horse and set her on her feet. Her knees immediately buckled, and she sat in the trail as her circulation returned to normal.

The horses were allowed to drink at a nearby stream and then began grazing on the grass. The men in the party went about the business of taking a break. Something told Enid she wouldn't have much time to relieve herself. She couldn't very well do so with her hands behind her back, so she mustered all of Sorcha's bravado and struggled to her feet before approaching her captor, who was eating what looked like a slice of fruitcake.

She spoke loudly so everyone in the party would hear; hoping one of them spoke English. "Please remove the bindings."

Her captor looked over at an older man, who said something. It must have been a translation, because her captor looked back at Enid and shook his head no.

"If you do not, I will be forced to wet my skirts and you will have to smell it for the rest of the trip," she declared.

The older man laughed and translated again. Her captor's face fell into a disgusted grimace, but he stuffed the rest of his meal into his mouth and fumbled with her bindings. All five men watched her closely as she went off the trail in search of a suitable spot to go. She was too desperate to be concerned that they could see her – besides, her skirts provided enough protection that they didn't see anything anyway.

She was surprised to find that the small knife she'd secreted away in her under-pocket was still there. Not that she had any intention of using it.

The older man who'd translated gave her a drink from his canteen and a small portion of his meal. It was a cake of dried meat and berries that she chewed and swallowed quickly. When her captor gestured that she should put her hands behind her back so he could bind her again, she balked.

Turning to the translator, she said, "Tell him I won't fight or try to escape. Please ask him to let me sit upright."

He obliged, and a minor argument ensued. Finally, a man with his hair singed on either side of his head in a traditional Mohawk snapped out what Enid took to be an order because all discussion ceased. With no humor in her heart whatsoever, she made a mental note that the Mohawk with the Mohawk was the boss of this operation.

Her captor set her upright on the horse and mounted behind her. He snarled something in her ear, and she understood the threat perfectly well without knowing what his actual words meant.

The afternoon passed more tolerably, although now that her physical discomfort had been attended to, her mental torment had free rein. Since the first ships made harbor on these shores, colonial girls and women had been stolen from their families and integrated into various Native American tribes. Enid knew she was now a slave. Whether her life would get worse or better remained to be seen.

Chapter Eleven

Sorcha

She woke to find Grammy Fay sitting on the side of her bed, patting her leg.

"I came in to check on you a few minutes ago," Fay said, "and you were crying again."

The skin of Sorcha's cheeks felt tight from dried tears. "It wasn't me. Enid cried herself to sleep."

"You are Enid." Fay's voice was soft and sympathetic. "What happened?"

In an unemotional voice, Sorcha gave her an abbreviated version of events while Fay rubbed the same spot on her leg through the bedspread until she thought she would scream. When she'd finished describing Enid's kidnapping, and before Fay could say more than, "Oh, Sweetling, how terrible for you," she slipped out of bed and went to stand in the bathroom doorway.

"I need to get a handle on this," she said. "I can't keep letting Enid disrupt my life. So please don't ask me any more questions…not today. Okay?"

Her grandmother gave her a sad smile and nodded.

Sorcha took her shower, fixed her hair and pulled on her clothes in a zombie-like trance. She wanted nothing more than to call Paula and cancel attending the football game, but if she didn't go, she'd sit around the house moping. She'd told Fay she didn't want Enid's life disrupting her own, so she'd best get on with it.

The game was scheduled to begin at 10:00 am, so she had a chance to catch up with her parents at the breakfast table. Her mom had simmered a batch of steel-cut oatmeal with cinnamon. Enid's gnawing hunger from the day before seemed to have transferred itself to Sorcha, because she devoured her portion and asked for more. The conversation was by necessity limited to Sorcha's life; her parents had never believed in Enid and never would. They had no idea she was still under the 'delusion' that Enid was real.

In the lane, Paula was uncharacteristically late. When she did arrive, Luanne was sitting in the passenger seat. Resignedly, Sorcha opened the back door, but to her astonishment, found Ben sitting behind Paula. She avoided eye contact, got in next to him and fastened her seat belt as Paula drove off. No one spoke for several seconds until Luanne turned around in her seat. The smile was absent today. "Hey."

There was a strange atmosphere in the car, like everyone but Sorcha knew something, and they were reluctant to share. She forced herself to say, "How's it going?"

Paula glanced over at Luanne and said, "Well, it's been an interesting morning."

Luanne had seemed so light-hearted the previous two times Sorcha had met her. Now her words, "We need to talk," sounded serious to the point of curtness.

Sorcha looked at Ben. His lip was no longer swollen, but the bruise under his eye had gotten darker. He was slumped slightly in the small space the compact car afforded him, and his knees came up almost to his chest. Today he had no charming smile for her; his manner was subdued.

"You told her," Sorcha said.

"I had to."

A scoffing little laugh escaped her. "Why don't you people stop beating around the bush and tell me what the hell this is all about?"

"We know who you are," Luanne said.

Sorcha met Paula's eyes in the rearview mirror, but this morning the warning look was noticeably absent.

Unsure, Sorcha said, "Paula?"

"I neither confirmed nor denied," Paula said. "But you need to listen to what they have to say."

Luanne shook her head. "Don't blame Paula. As soon as you mentioned Bear Talker to Ben, we knew."

"Suspected," Ben said.

"At least I always believed," Luanne retorted.

"Yeah, okay," he muttered, looking out the window.

Suddenly the convoluted conversations with Ben about Bear Talker made blinding sense. "Wait a minute," Sorcha said. "Your little secret society has something to do with…me?"

Luanne pressed her lips together and appeared to be considering her next words. "We have to be careful what we tell you."

Her meaning might seem obscure to anyone else, but Sorcha read between the lines: they knew things she didn't – about Enid's future.

"Oh," she said softly.

The very concept of someone other than her grandmother and Paula knowing about Enid, believing in Enid, was foreign to everything she'd learned to do to protect herself over the years. Just in case she misunderstood, she said, "Tell me her name."

Luanne didn't ask what she meant. She looked at her brother, who shrugged his agreement that it couldn't hurt.

"Enid," Luanne said.

Paula shot a quick look over her shoulder. "I didn't tell them."

"I believe you."

They'd reached the bus stop. Sorcha wondered where Luanne was going on a Saturday but didn't ask. Luanne got out but leaned inside and spoke to Ben. "They called a special meeting this afternoon. Make sure she's there." She shut the door and walked away.

Sorcha was too shell-shocked to even crawl into the front seat. She just looked at Ben, queasily wishing she hadn't eaten all that oatmeal.

"It's where Bear Talker's longhouse used to be," he said. "The meeting."

"Yeah, I kinda figured."

When they got to the school parking lot, he put a hand on Sorcha's arm to stop her from leaving. Paula gathered her things and left them alone in the car.

Ben sat up straight and studied her face until Sorcha began to feel uncomfortable. "What?"

"You don't look like her."

A thrill of something like excitement went through her. "You have a picture? No one's ever done a portrait of me – I mean Enid."

He winced. "So much for not telling you what you don't already know."

"Your sister said you didn't believe. Is that why you wigged out on me?"

"I didn't wig out." It was a weak protest. He looked down at his hands, clasped loosely between his open knees. "I was raised to believe in a story passed down through the generations for two hundred years. Didn't get all the details until I was old enough not to go around blabbing, but yeah, it's hard when you're asked to put faith in the impossible."

"I'd like to hear that story."

"Not from me."

"Then who?" She was getting frustrated.

"You have to live it." He gave her a rueful smile. "Look, I need to ask you something. What day is it tomorrow for Enid?"

She shrugged. "It's tomorrow, exactly two-hundred and thirty-six years ago."

His countenance didn't change, but his eyes flickered. Was that concern she saw?

"Why?" she asked.

"What was yesterday like for her?"

"Oh, you could say she had a pretty bad day."

"Just tell me, Sorcha."

"Really? Is that how it works? You and Luanne and your secret buddies come along and ask questions, order me around and I get nothing in return?" She reached for the door handle. "I don't think so."

She got out, slammed the door, and hurried across the dirt lot. The game had already started, so there weren't very many students around. He caught up to her just before she got to the pavement. "Sorcha!"

The loud growl of a rapidly approaching engine drowned out whatever else he said. She glanced around. John Nelson's jacked-up black truck was speeding down the aisle, straight for them. Ben threw his arms around her and dragged her between two cars. John, his head sticking out the window, pulled up and laughed raucously.

"WOO, Coz, you should see the size of your eyes!" he shouted. There was a strip of white tape over his nose, and both eyes had thin black streaks under them.

"Yeah? Get out of the truck and say that!" Ben yelled. Now it was Sorcha's turn to throw her arms around him – to prevent him from hauling John bodily out the truck window.

John popped the clutch and spun his tires in the dirt, sending rocks flying as he sped away. Ben's tense body leaned in the direction he'd gone. She realized her arms were still grasping him around the chest when he turned his head, bringing his face to within inches of hers. Her heart had already been racing from nearly getting run over, now it skipped a beat or two as his brown eyes looked into hers. She pulled away quickly, but later, when she was supposed to be watching the game, she remembered the intensity of the look and wondered what would have happened if she hadn't.

She and Paula sat several rows up from Ben, who was hanging out with the same group of kids he sat with at lunch. The teams were evenly matched for once and the game was exciting, but not as exciting as the unofficial half-time show. Kristin Barber and her cheerleading squad did their thing, shaking their pom-poms and riling up the crowd, but as soon as the last cheer rang out over the audience, Miles Blumenthal, quarterback and all-around team hero, stomped onto the field and grabbed Kristin by the arm. Sorcha couldn't hear what they were saying, but it was obvious from their gestures and furious faces that they were having a very public fight.

"Dang," Paula said, stretching out the word.

Sorcha looked around for Ben and caught sight of him down on the sideline talking to, of all people, Dalton. She had a moment of pure panic as it occurred to her that Ben knew how Paula felt about Dalton. All she could do was hope he kept his mouth shut. She was glad Paula was distracted by the spectacle on the field. Sorcha glanced over just in time to see Kristin slap Miles in the face. The crowd roared its approval.

"I love it when royalty shows its ugly side, don't you?" Paula had a big grin on her face.

Sorcha murmured an appropriate response, all the while watching Ben make his way back to his seat. He paused before sitting down to scan the crowd. She thought maybe he was looking for her but noticed him staring off at a group of young men who were flaunting the rules and smoking on school property. John Nelson was among them. He took a deep drag before flicking the burning cigarette butt in Ben's direction. Then he turned abruptly on his heel and walked towards the parking lot.

After the game, the question of how Sorcha was supposed to get to this big secret society meeting was answered by Paula.

"I offered to drive you if they'd let me attend," she said.

Sorcha was relieved. "Good. I mean, that you'll be there. You know all about Enid, so why wouldn't they let you go? I hope I get a straight answer about, you know, why this secret society started in the first place. It's logical to assume Enid tells someone about me…" she stopped. Enid already had told someone. Bear Talker – and Joseph. The thought made her hopeful for the first time that Joseph hadn't been dead after all.

She hadn't known what to expect from the meeting. Her mind conjured up everything from a Native American powwow dance around a bonfire to a midnight grove of masked, chanting men. Instead, it was a bright, cold afternoon and there were about forty men and women milling about or sitting in folding chairs arranged in two rows in a big circle. When she and Paula tentatively entered the grove of pines, everyone got up and came over to shake their hands and say hello.

Sorcha was nervous, and with all the new faces immediately forgot just about everyone's names.

Luanne came forward and said, "This is our mother – Ben's and mine – Janet." A petite, older version of Luanne clasped Sorcha's hand in both of hers and said, "I'm just tickled to meet you. You're so much prettier than I thought you'd be."

Ben had said he'd seen a portrait of Enid, so Sorcha assumed all the others, including Janet, had also seen it. She decided not to be insulted, though, and just said, "Thank you."

Janet gave her daughter a tremulous smile. "Your father would be so proud." To Sorcha, she explained, "He died a few years ago. I know he would have wanted to meet you."

Sorcha maintained her polite demeanor, but her nervousness increased. Ben's mother was looking at her with borderline worship in her eyes. It was freaking her out.

As person after person paraded by, one thing Sorcha noticed was that most of the men seemed to have nicknames. There was a Benjie, a Skip, a Doc, a Curly and a Slim, plus several more she couldn't recall. The other thing she was quick to pick up on was that the members of this 'secret society' of Ben's were all related to each other – which was why she was floored when John Nelson appeared before her with a smarmy smile on his face.

He lifted her limp hand, kissed it and said, "Look what the dog dragged in." His eyes flicked over to Ben at the word 'dog.'

She snatched her hand away and wiped the residual dampness off on her pants. "What are you doing here?"

"Oh, Cousin Ben didn't tell you, huh? Shock."

He started to say more, but Ben appeared and gave him a dirty look. "Watch your mouth, John."

John's smile didn't budge, but his eyes narrowed into calculating slits. "Maybe you should watch yours, O' Chosen One."

"That's enough!" The speaker was Skip, an older man who grabbed a handful of John's shirt at the neck and hauled him back a few feet. "Sit down. I won't have any trouble, you hear?"

John backed away with a cocky swagger, watching Sorcha and Ben the whole way. Ben said, "Come on," and led her to a chair in the circle next to where Paula was already sitting.

Sorcha sat on the cold plastic seat, feeling as if all eyes were on her – which, for the most part, they were. Only one person seemed to be distancing himself from the rest, an older man leaning against a tree who had white hair pulled back into a ponytail. His face was carved with deep lines, like a block of tarnished marble that had seen hard times.

"Who's that?" She pointed him out to Ben.

"My Uncle Harry."

"The homeless one?" Paula asked.

"Yep, that's Harry the Hobo. He's not a bad guy, just a little mental. There's one in every family." Ben looked over at John. "Or two."

As soon as everyone was seated, Skip stood. "Welcome. As you may have heard, we found our Enid."

Several people clapped and shouted their appreciation.

Skip continued. "We're also pretty sure who our Ben is," he gestured towards Sorcha and Ben, "but if any of the rest of you want a shot at it, she's easy on the eye."

There was laughter from the circle. Sorcha had absolutely no idea what he meant.

"Janet, if you would." Ben's mother stood up and began distributing a single sheet of paper to each person present. When she got to Harry the Hobo, he shook his head and she moved on.

"This is the protection detail schedule," Skip said. "Ben and John will shadow her at school to the best of their ability. Those of you assigned to the house must take precautions not to alert the family to your presence. We've trained for this, people, so stick to the program."

Sorcha had had enough. Her hand shot in the air.

Skip raised his eyebrows. "Yes, I know, Sorcha. You've got questions. I promise I'll answer as many as I can, but first I've got one for you. Do you know what a paradox is?"

Sorcha nodded. "Something that contradicts itself but is still true."

"Have you heard of the Grandfather Paradox? Where you can't travel back in time to kill your own grandfather because if you did, you'd never be born to travel back in time in the first place?"

"Um…sure."

"All of this," he gestured around the circle, "has to happen, because we know it already happened."

"And it's a paradox because it happens because Enid said it did," Sorcha said.

"Exactly."

"And you know more, but you can't tell me, because Enid didn't know about it, or at least she didn't tell anyone about it."

"You," Skip said, pointing at her, "are smart. That's good."

He spun around, clapped his hands and said loudly, "Alright! Luanne, our very own history expert, was able to positively identify Sorcha's house. We are one-hundred percent certain this is the real thing, people! I feel like I should say something profound about how belief can sustain us. If Sarge were here, he'd have us all crying like babies, but as most of you know, he ran afoul of the law again this week."

There were chuckles, affectionate headshakes and nods all around. Sorcha noticed the only one who didn't respond was John. He was too busy glowering at Ben.

"Sarge may be out of action, but he'll be a part of our salvation in spirit," Janet chimed in.

"That's right!" Luanne reached out and took her mother's hand.

Sorcha wondered what the heck she'd gotten herself into. Salvation? Were these people nuts? She looked at Ben, who kind of rolled his eyes and said quietly, "This day has been a long time coming. Some of my family members are a bit fanatical about it."

"Ya think?"

He leaned closer, his face serious. "No one asked you to prove yourself, did they? We believe that you have two souls and live two lives."

"Should I be grateful? Is that what you're saying? Because I gotta tell you, I can't fight the feeling that you all have some purpose for me that you plan to keep me ignorant of."

His eyes dropped, and she knew it was true.

The men and women stood and walked off or milled about in little groups; she'd missed Skip's last words dismissing everyone. He came over and squatted down in front of her chair. Like most the others, he had dark hair and bronzed skin, but his eyes were a striking blue.

Before he could say anything, she asked, "There's something Enid needs to do, isn't there? She obviously already did it, though, so I don't see how anything we do now can make any difference."

"Or…" Skip said with a raise of his eyebrows, "what we do now makes all the difference."

Sorcha sighed. "Paradoxes are a pain in the ass, aren't they?"

He smiled. "You said you had questions."

She shook her head. "Never mind. I highly doubt you'll answer any of them."

"You're probably right, and I'm sorry about that, but it can't be helped." He stood up and nodded to Ben. "Take care of her."

"I will."

Paula didn't have much to say on the way home. She seemed as stunned as Sorcha. She did point out that a car seemed to be following them, and before they turned onto the private lane to Sorcha's house, the driver pulled over and parked. The owner of the land across the main road had built and rented out several duplexes. Cars parked along that road all the time, so as long as her 'protection detail' kept a low profile, they wouldn't be conspicuous there.

Sorcha put her hand on the door handle. "I feel like my life is one unending episode of the Twilight Zone."

Paula gave her an encouraging smile. "And I'm over here just privileged to be your side-kick."

Sorcha laughed and took a swipe at her but sobered quickly. "After everything that's happened, I'm afraid to go to sleep tonight."

Paula nodded in the direction of the parked car. "They're here to keep you safe, remember?"

Sorcha pressed her lips together.

"Are they?"

Chapter Twelve

Enid

She woke up face down on the horse again. This time the band of Mohawk were travelling at a good clip, cantering across an open field. She lifted her violently bobbing head to let her captor know she was awake, and he responded by shoving her back down and shouting something angrily. His tone told her she'd better not struggle, so she didn't, even though every hoof striking the ground sent painful shockwaves through her body.

She consoled herself with the knowledge that even a fit horse couldn't maintain a canter forever. Sure enough, after what seemed like an eternity but was probably only half an hour, they slowed to a walk.

The group of men chatted good-naturedly among themselves in their language, which suggested to her they were near the end of their journey even though New York, where Joseph said they were headed, would by her calculations still be several days' ride south. Another hour or so passed before the sound of children's laughter and barking dogs reached her. From her upside-down position, she caught glimpses of dark-haired, dark-eyed boys and girls who'd come out to greet the men and were curiously scrutinizing her.

Joseph had told her they were Mohawk, but the Mohawk homeland was northwest of her village, not south. She wondered who these people really were, and assumed she was about to find out.

She heard a woman's voice then, "What is this? Is she to be allowed no dignity among us?"

The Mohawk brave Enid had ridden with dismounted, and just like the day before, pulled her roughly from his horse. Also like the day before, Enid's vision faded to black around the edges, and she collapsed. She was immediately surrounded by curious dogs, sniffing her warily, some growling a warning. Through the dizzy buzzing in her ears, she heard the woman gasp dramatically and then begin blasting the brave with irate words in another language.

"Enough!" It was the older man who'd translated the day before. "She is unharmed, and that was the agreement."

Enid's vision slowly returned. She licked her dry lips and looked up, squinting into the sun. The woman shouted at the dogs, and they scattered. Standing before Enid was a slim squaw with white-streaked black braids hanging forward on each side. Beside her worried eyes were deep laugh-lines that spoke of happier times. Enid hadn't seen her since before her brain was capable of forming permanent memories, but she knew her nonetheless.

"Mother," she said. The word was uttered without joy or surprise; Enid was too exhausted for emotion.

Bluebird fell down onto her knees and threw her arms around her. "E-ee," she murmured. "My baby."

Her mother pulled away just in time: Enid's back hunched as her mid-section contracted into a tight ball and she vomited the meager contents of her stomach into the dust.

"This is 'unharmed'?" Bluebird practically screeched. Enid didn't know what her mother did next because she was too busy dry heaving, but a canteen soon appeared in front of her face. She took it but was too weak and shaky to tilt her head back properly to drink. Bluebird's gentle hands helped her, her voice soothing. "Take small sips, E-ee."

Someone carried her into a dark place and laid her on a soft surface near the ground. The air smelled of spice, a strangely familiar scent. Enid's mother stuffed furs under her upper body to prop her up and then she spoon-fed her a thin broth that tasted wonderful.

"I am sorry you were treated so," she said.

"Where am I?" Her eyes had adjusted enough to the gloom to see that she was in a vast-seeming space: the interior of a longhouse.

"Among the Haudenosaunee people."

Enid knew from Sorcha's studies that the Haudenosaunee were the Iroquois Confederacy, six Native American nations joined together: the Mohawk, Oneida, Onondaga, Cayuga, Seneca and Tuscarora.

"Who were those men who captured me?"

Bluebird frowned. "Black Wolf was sent from New York to fetch warriors from his chief's village. He came through here on the way and I convinced my husband to trade with him. He should not have treated you so badly."

Enid didn't comment on the 'my husband' part. It made sense that her mother would remarry.

"You paid him to kidnap me?"

"Not kidnap! Rescue. If I could have, I would have taken you with me all those years ago, but your father would have hunted me down and killed me. Now I have protection."

Enid sat up, glad to find the dizziness gone. "So you sent Black Wolf to the medicine man to find out where our house was."

Bluebird smiled and nodded. She looked very pleased with herself.

Enid didn't know for sure what had happened, but she suspected Bear Talker had refused to tell the Mohawk where she lived and they'd attacked, motivated by whatever her mother's husband had promised them in trade. She didn't mention any of this to Bluebird, not because she was trying to protect her, but because it was speculation.

"You have not asked about Elizabeth," Enid said.

"Shall I ask about her? Just to show you I care? Because I do not." Bluebird's tone was full of bitterness.

Enid bit her bottom lip and found it to be severely chapped. She was torn between loyalty to Elizabeth and the need to please her mother. She became aware of other people moving about in the longhouse. One thin girl seemed to be hovering just beyond her mother's sectioned-off living area.

From her kneeling position by the bedding, Bluebird looked around, held her arm out and said something in her language. The girl moved nearer and took Bluebird's hand. As soon as the girl came close enough for Enid to see her clearly, she knew who she was.

"This is your sister," Bluebird said, and Enid wasn't sure to whom she was speaking.

The girl appeared to be ten or eleven years old and was a miniature version of Bluebird, from the clothes to the braids to the shape of her face. The girl said, "How do you?" and Enid got the distinct impression the English words were the first she'd uttered except in practice.

Enid subsided back onto the furs, not because her dizziness had returned, but because she was overwhelmed with uncertainty. How had her mother expected her to react to this bombardment? She'd had her torn violently from her home and brought to live among a strange people with strange customs. Did she think presenting her with a sister would make it all better? Enid saw the closeness between the two; their hands were still linked, and the girl leaned against her mother's shoulder. Something like jealousy flared in her heart, but she squelched it quickly. The girl had an open, friendly look on her face. If she could welcome Enid, essentially sharing the mother she'd had to herself her whole life, then Enid could find the strength to accept it gracefully.

"What is your name?" Enid asked.

The girl looked down at Bluebird, who enunciated, "Spotted Fawn."

Spotted Fawn repeated the English version of her name and smiled proudly at Enid, who couldn't help but respond in kind. Enid put her hand on her chest and said, "Enid."

"Ee-nid," Spotted Fawn said.

The next hour or so passed getting to know Bluebird and Spotted Fawn. Enid was acutely conscious of her state of dishevelment after the rough journey and finally asked her mother if there was somewhere she could go to freshen up.

"Are you able to walk?" Bluebird asked.

"Yes. I am well now," Enid replied, hoping it was true.

Bluebird grabbed up some items and held Enid's arm as she guided her out of the longhouse, trailed by Spotted Fawn. Outside, there were several more longhouses spaced some distance apart, and smaller domed wigwams here and there. Beyond the structures and the wooden palisade surrounding them, a wide field stretched into the distance, dotted everywhere with flat-topped mounds of earth covered with the remains of the corn crop. Elizabeth had told Enid the story of The Three Sisters, which gave spiritual meaning to the indigenous agricultural system combining corn, beans and squash. At least a dozen women and even more children were out in the fields picking over what was left of the harvest.

The day was crisp and windy, with dark grey clouds that blocked the sun periodically. The inhabitants of the village went about their business, but Enid felt their eyes follow her. A few women paused to call out pleasant greetings to Bluebird. Men were scarce; probably they were out hunting and fishing – or perhaps, like the men of Enid's own village, they'd gone to war.

"You may be my daughter, but to the people here, you are a stranger," Bluebird told her. "You must prove your worth before they will accept you. You must learn to speak the Haudenosaunee languages."

Enid nodded.

Several children ran up and spoke with Spotted Fawn as Bluebird led the way to a secluded place along a narrow, fast-flowing river. When they got to the bathing spot, Bluebird flapped her hands at the children, and they ran off giggling.

If Enid wasn't also Sorcha, she might have had a typical colonial woman's reticence about being seen in her undergarments. As it was, she didn't hesitate to strip down and step into the frigid water. It took her breath away when she squatted in a sandy depression that seemed to have been hollowed out for the purpose of bathing. She grabbed handfuls of sand and quickly scrubbed her skin and hair. It was a deeply chilling, painful experience, but when she'd dried off and dressed in the linen leggings and soft buckskin dress her mother handed her, the worst of the shivering began to subside.

The moccasins were too big, so she wore her own battered leather shoes. She gathered up her soiled garments and they went back to the longhouse as one of the drifting clouds sprinkled them with a fine powder of snow. Inside, Spotted Fawn shyly offered to comb her hair. More and more people came inside the longhouse as the afternoon waned. The fire pits that ran down the middle of the cavernous space were soon sending clouds of aromatic smoke up to the vents in the ceiling as family after family prepared their evening meal. Enid was not ignored; she saw many eyes directed her way, but her mother's privacy was respected, and no one intruded on their meal of steamed fish, beans and some kind of potato-like tuber.

"I was adopted into the clan not long after arriving here," Bluebird said. "My clan mother was a good woman and I have many sisters I will introduce you to tomorrow."

Enid was in the midst of a most foreign environment, surrounded by unfamiliar faces, sights and sounds, but felt strangely as if she'd come home. That is, until a stocky warrior walked in through one of the doors and headed straight for them. His legs were bowed outward, a condition Enid knew from Sorcha to be caused by rickets in childhood. Bluebird jumped up to intercept him, but he ignored her and stopped in front of Enid. His face was anything but welcoming.

"So this is the witch," he said.

Chapter Thirteen

Sorcha

It was Sunday, thank goodness. Sorcha lay in bed thinking about Enid's predicament – if it could be called that. The word seemed to suggest hilarity and hijinks, but there was nothing amusing about Enid's situation.

The man who'd burst the comfortable bubble Enid's mother had constructed around her turned out to be Bluebird's husband. He'd sat among them and allowed Bluebird to serve him, all the while glaring at Enid with suspicious eyes. He'd said very little before retiring for the night, leaving Enid to wonder how on earth her mother had convinced him to trade for her 'rescue.'

But that was Enid, and Sorcha was as determined as ever to push that world aside so she could live her life.

She breezed through her morning routine, dressing in her favorite not-for-primetime sweatpants and comfy oversized shirt. For some reason, she found herself plaiting her hair into a much-shorter version of the braid Spotted Fawn had fashioned for Enid.

There was a sticky note on the refrigerator from Fay saying she'd gone to church and that Sorcha's parents had gotten up early to go antiquing in a neighboring town. Sorcha ate her customary bowl of raisin bran and, despite her intention to ignore Enid, found herself scouring the Internet for information on the Haudenosaunee. She didn't learn much that she hadn't already known. Most of the tribes that made up the Iroquois Confederacy had sided with the British. Enid was now living among the enemy, in more ways than one.

The doorbell startled her. Even without knowing she supposedly needed protection, she would have taken the precaution of peeking out the window before opening the door. Ben stood on the porch; hands jammed deep into his jean's pockets. His bike leaned against the porch railing.

She turned the knob and flung the door wide. "Come in, O' Chosen One."

He grinned and stepped over the threshold. "You have no idea what that means, do you?"

"None whatsoever. And I have a sneaking suspicion you're not going to tell me, right?" She shut the door and gestured that he should hang his jacket on the rack in the entryway.

"If I told you, I'd have to kill you," he said. Under his jacket, he wore a black t-shirt that hugged his torso and emphasized the muscles of his lean frame.

She raised her eyebrows at him. "Ha, I doubt it. How can your family use me for their nefarious purposes if I'm dead?"

Did she imagine his reaction to that? Did he freeze in place oh-so-briefly before catching himself and moving casually into the living room? She suppressed a shudder of premonition.

He sat in the exact same chair Joseph had sat in, although now it was a prized antique worth thousands of dollars, so she said, "Don't sit there. My parents would have a spaz."

He popped back up. "Where are guests allowed to sit?"

"Is that what you are? A guest? Because I don't remember inviting you."

"Call me whatever you want, but you're stuck with me."

She flounced down on the couch and reached for the remote. He sat at the other end and said, "There's a good game on."

She gave him a derisive look. "Yeah, that's gonna happen."

She turned on the TV and started flipping through channels. He wasn't too shy to let her know which shows he'd be okay watching and they finally settled on the cartoon network.

Despite the dubious beginning, the morning passed amicably. His comments on the cartoons they watched made her laugh more than the shows themselves. She went into the kitchen on a commercial and brought out a bag of Doritos and some soft drinks. He had to move closer to her on the couch to reach the chips and she'd become highly aware of him – and aware that she was dressed in quite possibly the least sexy outfit on the planet.

By the time noon rolled around, the cartoons were aimed at the preschool audience, so Sorcha shut off the TV. She looked at Ben expectantly.

"Now what?"

He shrugged. "When's your mom and dad coming back?"

"Probably not 'til late. They do this all-day date thing once a month and then go out to dinner. My grandmother should be home any second now, though."

"Is she cool?"

"Depends on what you mean by cool. She's rockin' the whole granny thing, you know, except for the blue hair, but if you mean will she be okay finding you here on the couch with me, then I guess so, as long as we're not..." For reasons that were beyond her, Sorcha's mouth had taken his question and run aground with it. She felt the heat of embarrassment rise up her neck.

Ben gave her a cheeky grin. "Not what?"

She couldn't stop the smile that spread over her face, but elbowed him in the ribs and said, "Shut up."

Just in case he took her words to mean it was okay to make a move, she stood up and walked toward the kitchen. "You want something for lunch?"

He picked up the bag of chips and the cans and followed her into the kitchen. "Sure, I can always eat."

She pointed to two aluminum trash cans and said, "Recycle's on the left. How about grilled cheese?"

"Cheddar?"

"Of course."

He nodded his approval.

The sandwiches ended up having more than just cheese on them; Ben raided the refrigerator and brought out tomatoes and lunch meat and onions. He found a small frying pan and nudged Sorcha aside to sauté the onions in olive oil before tossing it all on the bread and grilling it.

She got a couple more sodas out of the fridge and popped them open. "Where'd you learn to cook?"

"Juvie."

She started to babble an embarrassed apology, but he laughed and said, "Just kidding. You should see your face."

"Funny. So what's the deal with you and John anyway? He's your cousin, but he's the reason you went to juvie, right?"

Ben handed her a plate with the perfectly grilled sandwich. He sat across from her at the table before answering. "I kind of feel like anything I say'll sound like an excuse."

She took a bite of her sandwich and rolled her eyes in pleasure. The taste sure beat Enid's dinner of bland fish and strangely textured vegetables. Around her mouthful, she said, "Well, you already mentioned you're a black belt."

"All the Bens are." He cut himself off and made a face that told her he'd said too much.

"The Bens...?"

"Forget it." He rushed on with, "Me and John have always had this competition thing going. When my dad died, Uncle Sarge – John's dad – was there for me, you know? That's when John started giving me a hard time. We used to practice martial arts together. Back then I was short and skinny and, I don't know, he used to tease me. Call me names and stuff. It got on my nerves one day and I said something to him that was – well, it was definitely not nice. Next thing I knew we were fighting for real. I don't even know how it happened—how I beat him so bad, but he ended up in the emergency room with a broken arm and the cops were called. He said I attacked him, and I think he did it to get me out of the picture. So he could have Sarge all to himself again."

"Sarge is the uncle who's in jail?"

"Yeah. He drinks, but if it wasn't for that, he'd rule the world. He's got a lot of charisma; the kind of guy people listen to."

She noticed his use of the word 'charisma' and wondered about it. Ben Webster was no dummy.

"That's what Skip meant, then?" she asked. "About Sarge having everyone in tears?"

Ben had taken a big bite, but he nodded.

Sorcha had gotten him talking, though, and didn't want the trend to end. "Does your secret family society have a name?"

He shrugged, swallowed his bite and said, "Can't tell you."

"Oh, come on."

He laughed. "No really. The name kind of gives everything away."

"How about an acronym then?"

He'd taken another bite and she waited patiently for him to chew.

"WPS," he finally said.

"If I guess right will you tell me?"

"No."

She wrinkled her nose at him. "Wimpy Poophead Society?"

He laughed again. "Yep. You got it. That's us."

A muffled thump from the living room had him on his feet in an instant. His face deadly serious, he put his index finger against his lips and moved silently toward the kitchen entryway.

"It's just my grandmother," Sorcha whispered.

But it wasn't. A figure dressed in camouflage pants, a brown jacket and ski mask appeared from around the corner, black pistol gripped in his extended right hand. Before Sorcha could scream, before Ben could even react, the intruder fired, squirting a thin stream of water right at Sorcha's chest.

"Bang, you're dead." The voice was familiar.

Ben's jaw clenched and he said through his teeth, "You're gonna wish *you* were dead."

The intruder pulled off his mask with a flourish. It was John, with strands of his dark hair stuck up all over his head from static. "Just proving a point, Coz. It was easy getting past the stake-out. Those guys are sitting in their nice warm car barely awake – and Sorcha, babe, you really should lock the front door after yourself…or was that your protector's doing?"

He looked pointedly at Ben.

Sorcha moved to Ben's side, not to offer solidarity, but to put a hand on his arm to keep him from taking a swing at John. "Not in the house, please," she said quietly.

"Anyway," John continued, "If I was a bad guy, guess who'd be dead right now?"

"All of us," Ben said. Sorcha didn't understand his meaning, but it was clear John did. He tucked the fake gun into his waistband like he was some kind of gangsta.

"Maybe, maybe not. Either way, I just proved you're not cut out for this, Coz. You're too trusting. I think the elders got it wrong. I'm the Ben, not you."

Sorcha had had enough. "What the hell are you talking about?"

From behind John came the voice of Grammy Fay, raised in anger, "Language, Sorcha! What's going on in here? Who are these boys?"

Fay entered the kitchen and stood next to John with her tiny fists on her hips. She was dressed in her Sunday best, a floral dress covered with a pink, hand-crocheted shawl. Despite the fact that John and Ben towered over her, she was the dominating factor in the room. Her demanding gaze went from John to Ben to Sorcha.

Ben moved closer to Sorcha, and to her surprise, slipped his arm around her waist and pulled her to his side. It was a move designed to stake a claim; a move Fay's discerning eyes wouldn't miss.

Sure enough, her eyebrows rose. "I think introductions are in order."

Sorcha felt her face burn and knew that to Fay she looked guilty of something. The last thing she wanted was to tell her grandmother about the WPS and her 'protectors.' She stammered, "It – it's Ben. This is Ben and that's John…um, friends from school. Guys, this is my Grammy Fay."

Fay looked even more suspicious. "Friends from school that you've never mentioned? Because what I just heard didn't sound too friendly."

73

Ben tried to help. "We're working on a project for…" he floundered, and Sorcha knew it was because he had no idea what her classes were.

"History," she finished for him. "I got a bad grade on a test and Mr. Lee offered me extra credit if I did some tutoring."

Fay's eyebrows, thinned to almost nothing because she plucked out the gray hairs, scrunched up. "That doesn't make sense. If you got a bad grade, you should be the one getting tutored."

Sorcha bit her lip, cursing her inability to craft a fast, convincing lie. Luckily, Fay's attention wandered. Her laser-gaze scanned the kitchen: dirty pans on the stove, knife on the chopping block resting in a puddle of tomato juice and seeds, half-eaten sandwiches on only two plates.

"John just got here," Sorcha said quickly. She put a pleasant look on her face and turned to Ben's cousin. "You want a sandwich?"

John hesitated, and Sorcha could tell from the scheming glint in his eye that he was debating his answer. If he stayed in character as the voice of dissent, he was about to blow their little charade out of the water. For whatever reason, however, he decided to play along. "Yeah, sure. History makes me hungry."

Ben let go of Sorcha's waist and moved toward the stove. "Uh, Mrs. Fay? Have you had lunch?"

The suspicion faded from Fay's features and she smiled. "Just Fay, dear and no, I haven't. Can you make me one without onions? They make me fart."

John snorted with laughter while Sorcha halfway expected her flaming face to set fire to her head, but Ben took Fay's blunt statement in stride. "Well, we wouldn't want *that!*"

Fay beamed with approval when he went to the sink and washed his hands. She moved to Sorcha's side and said softly, "What a nice boy. And cute!"

Sorcha looked past her grandmother and saw that John had overheard. He stared back at her blankly. After what John had done to get Ben sent to juvenile hall, it was clear he had little affection for his cousin. They were enemies with a common goal: the WPS and whatever it stood for.

The afternoon passed pleasantly enough. Sorcha trotted out the extra credit assignment on the battles of the Civil War Mr. Lee had given her. Ben and John pretended they were clueless and in desperate need of tutoring because Grammy Fay kept making excuses to come into the living room to check on them. The boys made such a game of it that several times Sorcha had to tell them surreptitiously to tone down the dumb act. They stayed long after the assignment was finished, though, and Sorcha soon realized neither was willing to leave while the other was still in the house. The competition between the two was almost palpable. Ben stuck close to her side, pretending, ostensibly for Fay's benefit, that he was more than a friend, but Sorcha felt it was due more to insecurity, as if he was afraid John would fill his empty space if he abandoned her for even a moment.

At four o'clock she finally kicked them both out, saying with barely concealed exasperation, "Thanks, guys, it's been great, but I can take it from here."

Fay's presence made it impossible for either of them to protest and they got up to leave, but Ben's self-imposed pretense as her boyfriend asserted itself at the door. He leaned his head towards hers and she thought he was going to say something privately to her. Instead, he kissed her on the lips, a light brushing of skin on skin that took her completely off guard.

"I'll see you later," he said.

She managed to nod, but it wasn't until the door closed behind them that she realized she'd stopped breathing. Fay, oblivious to any undercurrents, pounced.

"I realize you've got a lot on your plate, young lady, but really, you could have mentioned that you were seeing someone!"

Sorcha almost said, "I didn't know myself," but instead went with, "It was all rather sudden."

"Well, he's got my stamp of approval. I hope he doesn't hang out much with that John boy, though. Him, I have my doubts about. Did he have to contradict everything Ben said?"

"Did he?" Sorcha asked, distracted. She touched her bottom lip with the tips of her fingers. It had been such a little thing, just a soft, casual kiss.

For the rest of the evening, the kiss was on her mind. She thought about it when her parents came home earlier than expected with leftovers from their favorite Italian restaurant. She thought about it when she brushed her teeth and when she laid her head down on her pillow.

It was the first thing Enid thought of when she woke in the longhouse.

Chapter Fourteen

Enid

Her mother was sitting cross-legged next to Enid's sleeping furs. She pushed the hair back from Enid's forehead and said, "You still sleep until you wake."

Enid sat up and stretched her sore body. The furs were soft, but the ground underneath them was harder than the straw mattress she was used to.

"Yes," she replied.

Bluebird looked around as if ensuring no one could hear. "My husband, Walks Like a Moose, suggested I apprentice you to the Haudenosaunee medicine man. It will bring our family great honor."

Enid had thus far been convinced Bluebird's uncommon resolve to get her back had been motivated by love and a desire to save her from her father's callousness. She'd assumed it was an unselfish act and that Bluebird had convinced Walks Like a Moose to help her at the risk of alienating him.

Now all her thoughts of family closeness were dashed. "Apprentice?"

Bluebird nodded, her eyes shining. "If you please him, he may even take you as his wife. Then he would join our clan."

Sorcha's world intruded as the Twilight Zone theme song played slightly off-key in Enid's head. Despite her shock, despite the automatic rejection of her mother's proposal, Enid knew it would be illogical to protest. There was nothing she could do or say to sway her mother against this course of action. Enid knew better than to place the blame on Walks Like a Moose. The Haudenosaunee were a matrilineal society. Even though Bluebird had married into the clan, she had a voice in its decision-making. She saw Enid as a stepping-stone to power in the community.

"And if he does not like me?"

Bluebird beamed. "How could he not? You are pretty enough and younger than the other women who would have him, and you have a gift that they do not."

With a cold feeling of dread, Enid asked, "What gift is that?"

Her mother's head tilted to one side as she regarded her. "You said you still sleep until you wake. The Mahican medicine man told me your spirit was split in two, and when you were a child you talked of nothing else. What was her name? Your future self?"

Enid thought then not of Sorcha, but of her own future self. She could see her life as if it were laid out on a path before her. The Haudenosaunee medicine man would use Sorcha's knowledge of history to predict things that would give him advantages unavailable to other leaders. If Enid cooperated, she could rule by his side. If she did not, he would get the information out of her one way or another. It was a scenario that she had long dreaded and one that she had vowed would never occur. She was worth more than the future half of her soul.

"I do not remember," she lied. "Elizabeth told me the medicine man's story, but I have long since stopped pretending I had another life."

Bluebird's eyes widened and for the first time, Enid saw anger in her face. She'd been all gentleness and persuasion, but Enid had heard her screeching at Black Wolf and knew she was capable of more.

"Pretending? I hardly think so. The things you told me even as a child were quite astonishing. Surely you realize how such a gift could benefit you?"

Enid knew she had to tread very carefully here. Not only must she convince Bluebird she had no such gift, but she must do so in a way that wouldn't further anger her. Bluebird had obviously hung big hopes on Enid. The knowledge that she had an ulterior interest in her was a crushing blow, because Enid had fallen for her kindness. It would be a miracle if she managed to deflect this woman – this stranger's – fury.

"It would indeed be a great boon if I had ever had such a gift. However, I assure you, Mother, I was never in possession of a second soul. From what Elizabeth tells me, I was merely an imaginative child."

Bluebird's lips thinned to a severe line. "Then why do you not wake?"

"The village doctor says my brain was injured when I was born. He has seen many such injuries when a babe does not breathe soon enough. Most are bereft of intelligence; I was lucky to only have problems waking." No village doctor had ever examined her, but her mother did not know that.

Bluebird pressed a hand to her chest, her face the picture of appalled betrayal. "This is grave news indeed. Walks Like a Moose cannot present you to the Haudenosaunee medicine man if you have nothing to offer him. I must stop him, and quickly."

Enid's mouth fell open as Bluebird jumped to her feet and rushed out of the longhouse. She felt as if her body had transformed into a leaf that was caught up in a capricious wind.

With no instructions on what to do, she combed and replaited her hair and tidied her sleeping furs. There was nothing readily available for her to eat, but she was accustomed to that. She needed to relieve herself however and was glad when Spotted Fawn arrived. She didn't know how else to tell her half-sister what she needed, so she bent her knees and made a "Pssss," sound, which made Spotted Fawn giggle.

Outside, about half an inch of snow covered everything, and more was gently falling. Footprints were everywhere, but the people who'd been out and about yesterday were scarce, and those she saw were bundled up in their winter robes.

Enid was unsure how much, if anything, Bluebird had told her youngest daughter. She watched closely for any difference in Spotted Fawn's demeanor. The girl showed no obvious change in her manner and for that Enid was thankful, although she suspected it probably wouldn't last. She accompanied her half-sister outside the wooden palisade that surrounded the village and along a well-worn trail some ways into the woods, until the stench told her the latrine was near. It was a huge European-style trench dug downwind of the settlement and nowhere near the water supply.

Enid wasn't sure how to go about the business she had there and mimed as much to Spotted Fawn. The girl gave her a funny look but supplied her with dried corn leaves and demonstrated how Enid should use the crude facilities. There was nothing dignified about it, but at least there was no one else about, and Spotted Fawn walked far enough away to give her a measure of privacy.

When she was finished, she washed her hands with snow and headed towards Spotted Fawn, but something caught her eye. At the edge of a dense stand of low-growing hemlock trees behind the latrine, a man stepped into view. Enid's heart skipped a beat or two when she saw him. He was facing away from the latrine but could easily have seen her doing her business. She hurried on, hoping he was just politely waiting his turn, but something made her look back.

The man was dressed the same as all the other warriors. His hair was like Joseph's, except the shaved part had grown out into stubble that was as dark as Sorcha's dad's five o'clock shadow when he had a few days off from work. The man turned enough to show her his face and she gasped as he melted back into the shadows.

It *was* Joseph.

Enid caught up to Spotted Fawn. She bent and with her finger drew the shape of a mushroom in a clean patch of snow, then pointed to her eye to indicate she'd seen some. Then she drew the shape of a basket and made a cupping motion over the mushroom and back to the basket. She pointed at Spotted Fawn and then in the direction of the longhouse. Spotted Fawn lifted the front of her robes to indicate they could carry the mushrooms that way. Enid frowned and brushed a hand fastidiously down the front of the winter robe her mother had leant her. Spotted Fawn shrugged and made a face that clearly said, "Whatever," and ran off. As soon as she was out of sight, Enid sprinted to the trees.

"Joseph!" she whispered. He'd moved from the last location she'd seen him, but she knew he had to be near. There were no revealing footprints in the snow; he'd taken care to disguise them. "Come out!"

Sugar maples dominated this section of the forest, an area that probably got a lot of traffic during the spring when the tribe tapped the trees for syrup. The maples were bare now, but in summer they would block the sun, allowing the hemlock growing beneath them to get little sunshine. This particular stand of hemlock might be stunted, but it was a hardy evergreen species that formed a thicket large enough to provide shelter for any local animals brazen enough to live so near the human settlement. A hand brushed aside a branch and gestured her over. She hiked up the buckskin dress and dropped to her knees, crawling underneath and through the shrubs. Joseph pulled her inside, where the branches had been thinned to make a cozy space, with the flat, rounded hemlock needles layered thickly on the ground. Without thinking, she went directly into his arms, hugging him and exclaiming softly, "I'm so glad you're alive!"

He hesitated before returning the hug. She felt his chin brushing the top of her head and the warmth of his breath in her hair. In fact, his body radiated warmth, more so even than when he'd held her in the field. She pulled away, instinctively knowing something was wrong.

Both of his eyes were purple from the beating the Mohawk had given him. Again, it reminded her of Ben, but there was something else, a swollenness to Joseph's cheeks and under his chin that made her think of the mumps.

"Are you well?" she asked.

He didn't answer; just shook his head slowly, his eyes conveying deep sadness.

"Is it Bear Talker? Did they burn his longhouse? Was that the fire I saw?"

He still said nothing and after a moment it occurred to her, horribly, why.

"Open your mouth," she said.

He shook his head and pulled back.

"Oh, my God." She put her cold hands to his hot face. His hands rose and covered hers, holding them in place against his cheeks.

"Joseph," she whispered, tears forming in her eyes. "Let me see it."

He tried to shake his head again, but she insisted, "You need medicine. Open."

It was dark under the branches except for the small amount of filtered light coming in through the needles. Joseph tried to open his mouth, but the swelling prevented his jaw from dropping very far. She saw enough, though. The base of what was left of his tongue was so purple it appeared black. Someone, maybe even Joseph himself, had crudely stitched the wound closed, although if he'd done it, she couldn't imagine how he'd managed. His breath was foul, but not overly so. She hoped that meant there was no infection.

From outside, she heard Spotted Fawn calling, "Ee-nid!"

She dropped her head in her shaking hands for a moment to get a grip on the tumult of her emotions. She didn't have time to indulge them other than to acknowledge a bottomless hatred for the men who did this to him.

"I have to go, or they will come looking. Do you need food?"

He didn't shake his head yes or no, but she answered her own question. "Of course you do, you're feverish and you can't chew anything hard. I'll bring you something as soon as I can get away again. Oh, Joseph…"

Spotted fawn's voice sounded closer, "Ee-nid!"

Enid took his face in her hands again and very gently kissed him on the corner of his mouth. "I'll be back."

She poked her head out. There was no sign of Spotted Fawn, so she scrambled out of Joseph's hiding place. It was a great spot to conceal oneself so close to the settlement, since the putrid odor of the open latrine trench would keep people from lingering in the area.

Enid saw Spotted Fawn's back not far from the trees and scooted around to come at her from an angle that wouldn't give Joseph's location away.

"Hello," Enid said. The girl turned with a relieved expression. Enid walked with her to the picture of the mushroom she'd drawn in the snow, which was almost obliterated by the new flakes that had fallen in the intervening time. She pointed to the mushroom and then put her hands to her throat and stuck her tongue out. Spotted Fawn laughed, understanding her meaning that the mushrooms she'd supposedly found were not edible. As they walked back to the longhouse, Enid hoped Joseph hadn't seen her little pantomime and misinterpreted it.

Inside, there was no sign of Bluebird. Spotted Fawn sat on her furs and got to work on sewing something. Enid knew that under normal circumstances, everyone was expected to make themselves useful to the community for a large portion of the day. The women did the farming and household tasks while the men went out to hunt and fish. Bluebird hadn't given her a list of chores yet, so she casually snooped around. Most of the foodstuffs were kept in a central location and shared communally. Like the siding of the longhouse, the containers were made of bark and most of them held the corn and beans the women had grown and dried. Along with stone knives, clay pots, wooden bowls and cups, Bluebird had smaller wooden containers with bark lids that held dried berries and nuts. Enid snuck a handful of each into her pocket, which she'd tied around her waist under the borrowed dress. She found nothing at all that could be used as medicine for Joseph's severed tongue. The medicine man was probably in charge of the stores of healing herbs. Him, she wasn't about to go see.

There'd been a stand of black willow trees growing by the river, though. The small knife she'd taken from her father's house was still in her pocket. She grabbed up one of her mother's clay pots and mimed to Spotted Fawn that she was going to get some water. She anticipated Spotted Fawn would protest that there was plenty of water in the longhouse, so she quickly hurried away. The snow had stopped falling, but it was cold. In this world, it was often difficult to judge time, especially when the sun was hidden. Enid estimated her mother had been gone for over an hour, however, and she worried she'd run into her.

Her luck held out. Three older women were casting woven hemp nets out into the river, but they were concentrating and didn't pay her any attention. She found a young black willow tree that hadn't been stripped of its bark. Quite a bit of moss stained its trunk and limbs, but she found a clear patch of the driest bark she could and hacked away at it with her knife. Sorcha's research into herbal remedies for Elizabeth taught her that willow tree bark was an excellent source of salicin, the natural form of aspirin. She filled the pot with water at the river, grabbed up several good-sized rounded stones from the riverbed and went straight back to the longhouse.

Spotted Fawn was no longer alone. Another girl had joined her, and they were chattering away in their language as Enid built up the nearest fire, set the rocks in the middle of the blaze and rested the pot near the edge. She cut the bark up into smaller pieces and put it in the water. Once the rocks were hot enough, she scooped them out of the fire with a wooden spoon and deposited them into the pot. The tea would have to steep for a while. To keep busy until it was done, she offered to help Spotted Fawn with her sewing. The girls were interested in Enid's clothes and asked, through pantomime, if it was okay to try them on.

Enid was embarrassed that the clothes were so filthy, but the girls didn't seem to mind. They were at that age where play was being phased out for the responsibilities of womanhood. It happened so much sooner in Enid's world than Sorcha's. Trying on the clothes was both play and an exploration of their budding maturity. Enid hoped they grew tired of it soon, because she planned to tear her skirt into a blanket for Joseph.

She was anxious to get back to him. Anxious to make sure he hadn't been discovered, and especially anxious to ease his pain. She wished more than anything that she could sneak out at night and stay with him, but as soon as she fell asleep, she'd be a dead weight, a dangerous burden. Just like she'd been when the Mohawk caught him in the first place.

In her determination to keep her two lives separate, Enid had become adept at distracting herself from unpleasant truths, especially those that underscored the yawning chasm between Sorcha's world and this one. Nothing thus far in Enid's life had more brutally highlighted that disparity than knowing Joseph had had his tongue cut out because he'd helped her. Perhaps, more than just a punishment, it had been a symbolic warning for him not to say anything about her kidnapping. The Mohawk warriors would want to avoid retribution from the townsfolk – not that Enid thought for a moment it would be forthcoming. Her father would not bother to look for her. Jedediah would seek someone else to fill his dead wife's place.

Another girl, older than Spotted Fawn and her friend, came over and said something. Her tone indicated she was bossing the younger girls around, and sure enough, they got up and reluctantly followed the newcomer to a different area of the longhouse. It was the break Enid was hoping for. She immediately got her knife out and went to work cutting the stitching holding her skirt to the bodice of her dress. She also cut a smaller bit out of the bodice, into which she put the handful of nuts and berries and a leaf-wrapped bit of soft fish left over from last night's meal.

She worked quickly, conscious that her mother would surely return soon. When she'd gathered everything together, she left the longhouse again, fully expecting to be stopped and questioned. All the way to the latrine trench her heartbeat double-time. Just in case she was being watched, she skirted around the trench to the left and walked in a meandering circle, pausing now and then to pretend she was harvesting berries. Finally she made it to the trees and Joseph's sheltering thicket.

He was asleep when she crawled in. She set the pot of tea aside and unfolded the blanket she'd made from her skirt. When she laid it over him, he woke with a start and his hand shot out to grasp her wrist.

"It's me," she whispered.

For a moment, his fevered eyes had no recognition in them. Then his eyelids drooped, and he released her arm, subsiding back onto his bed of leaves.

"You need to sit up. I brought you some willow bark tea."

He struggled back up and tried to hold the pot, but his hands were shaking. She put her hands over his and steadied them, looking into his eyes the entire time. "Take a sip and hold it in your mouth for as long as you can. It will ease the pain and is an antiseptic."

He wouldn't know what an antiseptic was, so she clarified, "Remember when I told your uncle about tiny creatures that make us sick? This will help keep them away."

Joseph obediently drank from the pot, even though he struggled to swallow past the swelling and his efforts obviously caused him severe pain.

"I brought you some food. I know it will be hard to eat, but you must try, or you will become weaker. Will you promise to try?"

He closed his eyes and nodded once.

"I cannot stay. If I am missed, they will look for me. I do not know when I will come again. Keep the tea from freezing if you can. Drink three mouthfuls in the morning, midday and after the sun sets. No more or it will hurt here."

She pressed a hand to his midsection. In the back of her mind, she wondered at her own temerity. She couldn't seem to keep from touching him. Was it gratitude for his sacrifice, sympathy for his agony or something more?

After sticking her head out to make sure no one was there, she made a move to leave, but he stopped her. She turned back and found him staring into her face as if he wanted to memorize it. His expression was a mixture of shame and longing. Shame, she assumed, because he was a strong warrior who'd been brought low – he didn't want her to see him this way, didn't want to be reliant upon her. And longing, well, instinctively she knew what he wanted. She raised a finger and brushed at a spot of dried blood on his lip, then used the same finger to tenderly smooth out one of his eyebrows. He looked like hell, but all she wanted was to throw herself into his arms.

He was gravely injured, though, and could endure only the mildest of contact. She leaned forward and ever-so-softly rested her cheek against his. "Thank you for trying to protect me," she whispered in his ear.

It was the wrong thing to say. He pulled back, looking hurt and affronted, but she said quickly, "No, Joseph, it is more than gratitude that I feel. Don't think that it is not."

Even as she said the words, she realized they were true. His eyes dropped to her mouth and he made a small sound in his throat. Her eyes closed briefly and when they opened, his face was very close, his breath tickling her lips. He rested his forehead against hers and they stayed that way for a minute or more. She couldn't stop her tears.

Finally, she said, "I want to stay, but I cannot."

He nodded, his forehead rubbing up and down against hers.

"When you are well, we will escape together. That is what I wish."

He moaned a little and tilted his head to meet her lips with his, more fiercely than could possibly be good for him. She allowed herself to enjoy it only briefly before turning her head away.

"Don't. I know it must hurt."

He laughed, a sound that could be produced without a tongue, and shook his head. He was telling her the pain was worth it, and she smiled back through her tears.

It took all her strength to leave him. As she walked the same meandering path as the one she'd taken to find him, she felt his eyes follow her. She only looked back about a dozen times.

At the longhouse, her mother was waiting.

"Where have you been?" she demanded. Then she appeared to soften, "Have you been weeping?"

Enid's eyes felt sore and she realized they must be red. She thought fast. "I was betrothed, did you know?"

Bluebird's face hardened again. "And you miss him? Love has no place in marriage. I loved your father, and I got his fist in my face as payment. Tomorrow the medicine man will see you. He will discover for himself how many souls you possess."

The defiance with which she said it told Enid she no longer believed her story. Enid, like Sorcha, was a terrible liar. She dreaded tomorrow, like she was beginning to dread all tomorrows.

Chapter Fifteen

Sorcha

Joseph's eyes were burned into her soul. Sorcha saw them when she woke, a brown so dark they appeared black when the light was low. As the light had been inside the shelter of the thicket. She saw them when she showered, how he'd had a single unshed tear trapped in his lower lashes when Enid left him. His face may not be handsome, but he had the best eyes…they would help him convey emotion where his voice would fail him.

She completed her morning routine by rote, but quickly. Her parents had already left on their long commute, and Grammy Fay appeared to be sleeping in. Sorcha skipped breakfast so she'd have more time to do some research on her father's computer.

There was surprisingly little information on the Internet about tongue injuries, or at least ones as severe as Joseph's. Most of the articles she found dealt with simple bite wounds, but she was partially reassured when she read that they rarely got infected and the tongue tended to heal quickly. There was nothing more she could do for him in Enid's technologically lacking world. She did find hope in an article about aglossia, which said that people who were either born without a tongue or had to have it removed often compensated for its loss by using other structures in their mouths to produce adequate speech.

Still, it depressed her, the thought that she'd inadvertently caused him such great pain. He may be able to overcome the worst of it in time, but his life had been forever altered. She wondered if his parents, who'd taught him such good English, had also arranged for him to learn to read and write. It wasn't as uncommon as people might think for a Native American in those times to be literate; many tribes had converted to Christianity and were motivated by trade to work with the Europeans who were slowly and inexorably invading their territory. If Joseph could write, he had a way to communicate with anyone who could read.

When she went outside to meet Paula, she felt disoriented at first that there wasn't any snow. It had been a long time since Enid's world had encroached upon Sorcha's enough to confuse her. She was not surprised to see Luanne in the front seat and Ben in back. He smiled at her when she got in, but Sorcha found she couldn't even force a polite response.

"Everything okay?" Luanne asked.

They drove past a parked car with partially frosted windows. The two occupants waved at Luanne. It was a little thing, but for some reason seeing the protection detail lurking like vultures waiting their turn at a carcass set Sorcha off.

"No, everything is not okay. Why would you even ask that? Everything is really freaking not okay."

Ben put a hand on her knee, and she turned on him, aware of the peevishness in her voice but unable to stop herself. "Are we still playing boyfriend and girlfriend? Because I don't remember agreeing to that. Stop pawing me and stop…stop looking at me with Joseph's eyes!"

To her mortification, she burst into tears. Ben immediately made a move like he was going to put his arms around her, but she shook him off and said incoherently, "Nuh!" She turned away and bent nearly double, arms hiding her face. Her skin felt like it was too tight under her clothes, like she was encased in a suffocating cocoon, compressing her entire being until her heart felt like it was going to explode from the pressure. She couldn't breathe; the sobs came out in quick, gulping gasps. If asked to put into words exactly what she was crying about, she wouldn't have been able to comply except to say, "Everything."

After a while, the sobs subsided into shallow, shuddering breaths. She straightened up slowly, too wrung-out to care what she looked like. A handful of tissues was suspended in front of her face. Luanne, the practical one, trying to be helpful.

Paula had parked near Luanne's bus stop, but since Luanne hadn't gotten out Sorcha took it to mean she was waiting for the tear-storm to pass so she could ask – or tell – Sorcha something.

Sorcha snatched the tissues and said shortly, "What?"

"Tell us about Joseph," Luanne said.

Sorcha blotted her face and blew her nose, gathering her thoughts. The intense look on Luanne's face told her how important the information was to her. Perversely, it only made Sorcha want to clam up. She suspected they already knew about Joseph, though, and maybe if she just told them what they wanted to hear, they'd back off and give her some space.

"He's a Mahican man who tried to help Enid. Mohawk braves cut out his tongue."

Her voice broke and tears began to form in her eyes again. She pressed the wad of damp tissues to her eyes impatiently.

"When?" Ben asked. "When did they do it?"

He didn't ask why, just wanted to know when. She remembered before when he'd asked her what day it was for Enid. She'd told him Enid was exactly two-hundred and thirty-six years ahead of her to the day, yet here he was still asking when. Then it occurred to her.

"You don't know exactly when things happened, do you? That's why you need me to tell you."

She saw confirmation in his face. They had a chain of events, but no timeline.

"So something's going to happen, but you aren't sure when?" It was a shot in the dark; that she might catch one of them off guard enough to confirm what she suspected.

Luanne didn't bite. "You know we can't tell you."

Sorcha released a shuddering sigh. "Fine. Enid brought the medicine man, Bear Talker, to see Elizabeth the day before she died, and that's when she met Joseph, Bear Talker's nephew. Joseph was attacked the day she was kidnapped, so that would be her Saturday morning."

"Poor Joseph," Paula murmured.

Sorcha looked over and the sympathy on Paula's face reactivated the tears. "They cut out his *tongue* and he still came for her."

Paula's eyes widened and an unspoken question hovered in the air between the two friends. Sorcha's lips turned down at the corner and she nodded slightly, sending an unspoken answer: *Yes, I care for him.*

She glanced at Ben and caught a quickly hidden expression, like he'd eaten something that didn't agree with him and it had just come back up to surprise him. She didn't have time to contemplate it since Luanne shifted in her seat and opened the car door.

As she always did, she leaned in for that final word. To Ben, she said, "Don't screw this up." To Sorcha, she offered, "I know this is tough for you, but don't do anything stupid, okay?"

Like what? Sorcha thought. The past had already happened.

After Luanne gently shut the car door, Paula pulled back onto the road and drove to school like it was just another day. No one said anything. When Paula parked, Ben didn't try to stop Sorcha when she got out. She and Paula walked together, with Ben following several paces behind. Sorcha left Paula at their locker and went straight to the restroom to splash water on her blotchy face. Then she went to her first class and did her best to focus on the teacher and his lecture. When lunch came around, she sat on the stage with Paula, nibbling on the crackers and cheese she'd tossed into a bag that morning. By unspoken agreement, they made small talk about Halloween, which was only a few days away.

Sorcha tried not to look for Ben but found her gaze searching the crowded gymnasium again and again. He was absent for the first half of the lunch hour, and when he finally appeared, he sat with his friend at the table in front of the stage. For the first time, his back was to her.

If he was trying to get her attention, he was succeeding, and it irritated her. She'd been distant in the car because she was still so raw from Enid's feelings for Joseph. Plus, Ben's assumption that she would welcome his attention was annoyingly arrogant. Even so, and even though it had only been a few days, she'd become accustomed to the idea that he was *her* Ben. And now he was ignoring her.

She remembered what Skip had said, "We're also pretty sure who our Ben is, but if any of the rest of you want a shot at it, she's easy on the eye."

At the time, his words had baffled her, but since then Ben's attempts to get close to her made it clear it was just another bit of information the WPS had about Enid. Sorcha figured that one day Enid would tell someone in her world that Sorcha...what? Had fallen in love with a guy named Ben? Despite her attraction to him, it was hard for her to even consider the idea. Her heart – Enid's heart – seemed set on Joseph. It felt wrong for her to want to be with both of them.

And yet, that had always been more than a possibility – that she would love a man in each of her worlds. Had it only been a week since she'd been confronted with the certainty that Enid would marry the odious Jedediah? Just the thought of being intimate with that man had made her sick. Sorcha suspected it would have colored her future relations with men in this world as surely as if she'd been raped. Was that why Enid had been so eager to become romantically involved with Joseph, a man she hardly knew? Or was it merely the prospect of him saving her and taking her away from all the people who wanted to own her: her father, Jedediah, her mother, and quite possibly, the Haudenosaunee medicine man?

It was all so confusing when Sorcha tried to justify her feelings – and keep them separate from Enid's.

"What's his deal?" Paula asked.

Sorcha had been lost in her thoughts and assumed Paula was referring to Ben. She started to say, "He's just playing hard to get," when she noticed Dalton Boyle and a couple of his friends were sitting with their legs hanging off the edge of the stage not far from them. He was wearing his football jersey and he and his buddies were laughing too loudly.

"Oh, God. Is he trying to start something with Ben again?" Sorcha asked.

Ben didn't even turn to look at Dalton, but at the next table down, Kristin Barber sure did. She had her blonde hair up in a perky ponytail today and when she stood, Sorcha wondered if she'd had her jeans specially spray-painted on. She sauntered down the aisle and just about everyone in the vicinity watched to see what she would do. They all knew Kristin had recently broken up with Miles, the quarterback who'd fought with her so publicly at Saturday's game. Dalton would be a fool to flirt with her, since Miles was his teammate and rumor had it he hadn't taken the break-up very well.

Sorcha saw the eager look in Dalton's eyes – and the miserable one in Paula's. She started stuffing the leftovers from her lunch into her sack, fully intending to drag Paula out of the room so she didn't have to witness the oncoming train wreck. To her surprise, Kristin's destination was a little short of Dalton. She stopped next to Ben's table and leaned her hip against it.

"Hey, Ben."

Kristin's voice was a throaty purr, but it carried in the near silence. Sorcha clenched her jaw and muttered through her teeth, "Oh, no she didn't."

Before she knew it, she'd abandoned Paula and her lunch, jumping off the stage to stomp over and grab Ben roughly by the back of his hoodie. A few insistent tugs to the fabric and he got to his feet.

"Let's go, Romeo," Sorcha heard herself say. She pulled him past an astonished Kristin and marched him in front of her down the aisle and out the door.

In the hallway, he looked over his shoulder and asked mildly, "Where we goin'?"

His eyebrow had disappeared under the lock of hair on his forehead and he had a grin on his face, an infuriating one that made her want to grin back at the same time she wanted to strangle him. She let go of him and stood there awkwardly as he turned to face her, tugging his hoodie back down into place. Her cheeks had been burning the entire trip across the gym and now she felt them reignite under his amused gaze.

"So are you still mad at me?" he asked.

"I wasn't mad at you."

"Coulda fooled me."

"I was upset," she said, "but not with you. Did you not hear what I said about Joseph?"

"That I was looking at you with his eyes? I heard. Didn't make sense."

"Not that. The part about him having his tongue cut out because he helped Enid. It was horrible, you can't imagine. She felt so guilty."

"Do you love him?"

The question came out of the blue and took her aback. After a few seconds, she responded, "Enid thinks she might."

He grimaced. "You *are* Enid. Why do you talk like she's not you?"

"You live two lives and tell me how you'd handle it," she snapped. She started to turn away, but he let out a groan of capitulation and threw his arms around her, drawing her close. She struggled a little, but he tightened his hold and said against her hair, "Just stop, okay?"

She did stop, suddenly aware that other students were in the hallway. The fifth period bell was about to ring.

He ran his hand down her back and up again, a soothing caress. "I just – I'm trying to understand how you could feel that way about someone you just met."

"Enid just met him. And her world is this…intense place. Things we see in the movies happen in her world for real. It's not like here and now." Even as she said it, she realized the here and now felt plenty intense pressed up against his body.

He inhaled and let it out slowly. "I never thought I'd be jealous of a man who's been dead for two hundred years."

She used his own logic against him. "How can you be jealous when you only met me a few days ago?"

He relaxed his hold enough to look into her face. "I grew up loving you. I wanted it to be me."

His confession took her breath away, but she managed to say, "I thought you didn't believe."

His grin reappeared, but now it was sheepish. "It's like religion: when you're raised to believe in something, it sticks whether you think it makes sense or not."

The bell rang, and students began pouring from the gym into the hallway. Ben released her and backed off, shoving his hands into his pockets. He was staring into her face in exactly the same way Joseph had – as if he wanted to memorize her features. The constant reminders of Joseph were beginning to blur the two together in her mind. It haunted her how they were so different and yet strangely similar.

Sorcha didn't know if it was this similarity, or the expectant look on Ben's face, or the fact that Kristin Barber was walking towards them with her nose in the air, but she acted on impulse and stepped close to him.

"I'll see you after school," she said, and brushed his lips with hers in just the same way he'd kissed her yesterday, lightly, like butterfly wings. The last glimpse of him before she walked away should have reassured her, but it didn't. He looked pleased enough, but it was mixed with something else, a wariness that hadn't been there before.

She did her best to concentrate in her last three classes, but the wary look on Ben's face bothered her. He'd just declared his love for her, and then the second she makes a move to reciprocate, he backs off? Although to be fair, all he'd admitted to was having a schoolboy crush on her – and not even her, really, just the legend of her. Just like Dalton for Paula, she doubted the real thing could possibly live up to Ben's expectations. Especially after she'd lost control in the car this morning.

After school, she waited for him with Paula under the flagpole. The flags hung limp in the cold, stagnant air. In the distance, a haze of fog and smoke particulates partially obscured the hills.

"You're not going to believe this, but Kristin spoke to me in Art Class today." Paula made jazz hands like it was a big deal.

"She apologize for putting paint on your chair?"

Paula scoffed. "Yeah, like that's gonna happen. But actually, she kinda surprised me. Told me she thought Dalton likes me."

Sorcha's mouth dropped open. "No way."

At Paula's raised eyebrows, Sorcha hastily amended it to, "I mean no way Kristin said it – not no way Dalton likes you."

"Well, we both know it's not true. She's ignored me since she moved here, and the day you happen to thwart whatever skanky plans she has for Ben, suddenly I'm not invisible anymore?"

Sorcha studied Paula's profile. Her nose was tilted up at the end, just slightly. It made her look younger than her almost-seventeen years, and very vulnerable. "You know, it's not that far-fetched that Dalton would like you."

Paula gave her a knowing look. "Kristin wanted to start a conversation with me so she could ask about you and Ben. Transparent much?"

"Did she? Ask about us."

"Nah. All I had to do was ask her about that tube of paint and she decided she had other things to do."

Sorcha nodded approvingly. "That's my girl."

Ben joined them. He glanced at Sorcha, the corners of his lips turned up in a small smile. "What's up?"

They started walking to the car and Paula said, "Oh, someone told me Dalton Boyle likes me."

"He does," Ben said.

Paula stopped and looked at Ben like he'd sprouted a second head. "What?"

"I talked to him at halftime at the football game. Told him I was sorry for splashing him, he said sorry for getting in my face about it and then he asked if I was sitting with you." Ben shrugged. "It was pretty obvious."

Paula's cheeks had gone pink during Ben's story. "What were his exact words?"

Ben rubbed the side of his face. "Uh, I don't know. 'Are you sitting with Paula and Sorcha'?"

"Okay, so he said Paula *and* Sorcha. What makes you think he wasn't interested in Sorch?"

Ben's eyes flicked over to Sorcha, a silent plea for help. She didn't know what to say. Unless he could offer more solid proof, she didn't want to encourage him. It was safer to be skeptical, so Paula didn't get let down.

Ben shrugged again, only this time his shoulders stayed up for several long, defensive seconds. He was clearly having a deer-in-the-headlights moment, so Sorcha let out a huff of impatience and pushed past him to link her arm with Paula's. She and Paula started walking again, heads bent towards each other, talking in excited but hushed voices.

"I was only trying to help," Ben's plaintive voice followed them.

At the car, Sorcha sat in the passenger seat and relegated Ben to the back. He muttered, "I see how it is," but it was good-natured. Sorcha noticed he didn't say a word during the drive, just listened as she and Paula discussed Dalton, dissecting every possible nuance of the evidence for his liking Paula.

When they got to Sorcha's house, a 'protective detail' car was already waiting at the entrance to the lane. Skip was leaning against the hood and he gestured to Paula to pull over. Ben rolled down his window and asked, "Where's John?"

"He called and said he got detention this afternoon. Dumbass. Are you going to hang out at Sorcha's?" He bent and looked into the car. As an apparent afterthought, he said, "Hi, Sorcha. Paula."

After the girls returned his greeting, Ben directed puppy-dog eyes Sorcha's way and said, "I was hoping I'd get invited."

She laughed and obliged. "Ben, would you please hang out with me this afternoon?"

Ben gasped and put his hand to his chest like he'd just won an Academy Award. "I'd love to," he said in a high-pitched voice.

Sorcha and Paula giggled, but Skip reached into the car and thumped him on the side of the head. "Don't forget what we're here for."

92

Ben sobered instantly. "As if I would."

Skip nodded. "Remember, I'm all by myself tonight. We need someone watching the entrance to the property at all times, so I won't be conducting a perimeter check."

Sorcha hadn't known the WPS had been prowling her father's property. "What kind of a threat are you expecting? Shouldn't you at least give me a hint about what to look for?"

Skip's face fell into that rueful look she was beginning to expect whenever she asked him anything. He sucked air though his teeth and said, "Sorry, can't say."

She didn't know if he couldn't say because he didn't know, or if it was because of the paradox, but her irritation with the whole situation flared again. "Fine. I'll keep an eye out for anything and everything. Is the threat bigger than a breadbox? Bigger than Godzilla? Or is it too small to see? Should I be wearing a Hazmat suit?"

Skip wasn't fazed by the barrage of sarcasm. "Just stick with Ben and don't take chances."

She wondered what chances she was supposed to avoid taking in her own house but closed her mouth to prevent the next retort. Skip was only doing what he felt was best. She tried to summon up some gratitude, but all she could come up with was a weak, "Alright. Thanks."

To Ben, Skip said, "My relief comes at seven, so if you want a ride home, you better be here."

"Yes, sir."

Skip stepped back and saluted; his way of declaring the conversation over.

When Paula pulled up in front of the house, Sorcha invited her in, but she declined. "Can't. I'm babysitting tonight."

It smelled like cookies inside the house. Grammy Fay was in the kitchen, and she smiled when she saw Ben. "Oh, look who's here! Just in time for a fresh batch."

She held out a plate of oatmeal cookies and Ben took one but eyed it suspiciously. "I don't want to sound ungrateful because these look awesome, but are those raisins?"

"No, no, dear, those are chopped up dates. Better than raisins."

He held the cookie in front of his mouth and said, "Well if by 'better' you mean 'similar,' I have to warn you: raisins make me yak."

Fay looked at her granddaughter for interpretation.

"Barf," Sorcha said.

"Oh. Well, then here," Fay took the cookie out of Ben's hand and went to the counter. She selected another one and gave it to him. "These aren't hot, but it's just chocolate chip. Those don't make you yak, do they?"

By way of answer, Ben shoved half the cookie in his mouth and gave her a thumbs-up.

"Oh, my," Fay murmured. "I think you're going to need some milk to wash that down."

While Fay opened the refrigerator, Sorcha leaned close to Ben and said softly, "So you think we're going to see anything more threatening than raisins tonight?"

"Dates," he corrected. "And I hope not."

After they consumed two cookies and a glass of milk each, Sorcha pushed Ben into the hallway. She handed him a pair of gloves.

"These are my dad's, so they should fit you."

He watched as she bundled up in a matching black-and-white checkered hat and scarf.

"I take it we're going out?"

"There's something I want to show you before it gets too dark."

It was only four o'clock, but the days were getting shorter and combined with the overcast sky, it seemed much later. Sorcha led Ben through Grammy Fay's greenhouse, where she snipped a few more roses from one of the bushes. Ben inspected a row of lush, green herbs growing in little pots and said, "Cool." He plucked a leaf and rolled it between his fingers, inhaling the scent the crushed leaf left behind.

"Next time I cook for you, I'm coming here first," he said.

"Come on." She hooked her arm through his. They crossed the yard and went out the back gate.

The knee-high wild grass was turning yellow as it went dormant in preparation for the winter. They walked past the grove of oaks and Sorcha realized with a pang of guilt that she'd barely given a stray thought to Aggie, Bess and the children. Not that there was anything she could do if their fate had been as gruesome as Joseph's.

She shuddered at the thought.

"Are you cold?" Ben asked.

"No, just thinking."

"About?"

"The day Enid was kidnapped, the other members of the household hid in that oak grove. There were children she was responsible for. I don't know what happened to them."

94

Ben glanced over at the trees. "Seems like a good place to hide. I'm sure they were fine. Probably grew up and got married and had twelve strapping children each."

She looked at him in wonder as his comment sparked a sudden insight. Grabbing his hand, she pulled him along behind her as she ran the rest of the way to their destination: the graveyard.

Her intention had been to replace the flowers on Elizabeth's grave, but instead she went straight to a marble headstone three plots over. It was one of the earliest of the stones still standing, and one that had been a perplexing puzzle for Sorcha as she'd identified each of the cemetery's other inhabitants. She assumed the occupant, like all the rest, had been a relative, but she hadn't been able to find any records.

Ben came to stand next to her. "Who's Sarah Murphy?"

"I never found out. A fire destroyed all the birth records in the village before 1800 and Sarah has been a mystery. But the children I mentioned? The little girl's name was Sarah."

Sorcha had written down the epitaphs for each of the cemetery's headstones. The mysterious Sarah's stone had no birthdate, but it did show a death date of 1832. Jedediah's daughter had been around six years old in 1776, so if this was her final resting place, she would have been sixty-two when she died, a reasonable lifespan for the times.

Sorcha looked around even though she already knew none of the stones bore Sarah's brother Ezekiel's name. But just because he hadn't been buried here didn't mean anything. If Jedediah had been killed in the Battle of White Plains, the children would have been orphaned. Had Fergus adopted them? Given his nature, it seemed unlikely, but if Enid managed to escape the Haudenosaunee with Joseph, she could have had a hand in convincing her father to keep the children on. It was more than a possibility; Sorcha was certain now that the long-dead Sarah Murphy was the same scared little girl Enid had met just a few days ago. If Sarah had grown up in town and gotten married, she would have taken on her husband's name. Sorcha resolved to get online as soon as she got back to the house to research Sarah through her maiden name, which was presumably Johnson, the same as Jedediah.

Ben pointed to a phrase inscribed at the bottom of Sarah's headstone. "That looks like Algonquian."

"Yeah, I'm pretty sure it is. Mahican, probably," she said. "That word means 'two,' or at least I think it does. My grandmother spoke the language, but she couldn't write. Enid tried asking her but didn't know how to pronounce any of the words."

"You try online?"

She shot him a sidelong look. "Of course I did. No one speaks it anymore and it's not like there's a free online translator. I'd have to pay for someone to translate it for me."

"Well, my uncle Harry speaks several Algonquian dialects. If we can find him, you could ask him, or Luanne could help," he said. "She'd probably drool all over this place."

"Yeah," she said absently, her mind winging ahead to the planned Internet search. Sarah Johnson was a very common name. Even with a death date and location, the search would be time-consuming. Sorcha bent and ran her fingers over the stone, feeling the roughness where the chisel had chipped it away to reveal the letters. There were any number of reasons why Sarah's loved ones might have had Native American words inscribed on her headstone, but none that came to mind.

She shrugged off her thoughts and went over to Elizabeth's grave. The flowers she and Fay had placed there had either blown away or were withered and sad. Sorcha tossed the remaining blossoms aside and replaced them with the fresh ones. Ben came and stood next to her.

"Elizabeth," he said. "That's your grandmother."

Reflexively, Sorcha opened her mouth to say, "Enid's grandmother," but a sharp, loud report sounded from the vicinity of the oak grove.

Gunfire.

Ben threw his arms around her and dragged her to the ground, keeping himself between her and the trees. "Get behind the tombstone!" Elizabeth's stone was too small to provide adequate cover; Ben shoved her towards the closest one that would.

She crawled rapidly along the moist ground, elbows churning the dirt like a marine in training, Ben on her heels. The stone they were headed for was crowned with the statue of an angel. It belonged to Sorcha's great-great-grandmother Ruth, and as they hunkered behind it, she silently thanked the unknown relative who'd sprung for such a large, ostentatious monument.

"Is it a hunter?" Sorcha's voice shook. She clutched Ben's arm. "It's hunting season – he's probably not even shooting at us."

Another shot rang out, immediately followed by one of the wings of the stone angel taking flight and ricocheting off the gravestone directly in front of them.

"My mistake!" Sorcha buried her face against Ben's shoulder.

"He's going to circle around, and we'll be sitting ducks," Ben said grimly. He snatched the distinctively patterned hat from her head and put it on his own, then yanked her scarf off and tied it so the ends hung down his back.

"Stay here. Stay close to the ground." The words were uttered between clenched teeth. "Don't you dare move, do you hear me?"

She started to nod when she realized belatedly he meant to draw the gunman's fire by pretending to be her. She reached a hand out, saying, "Ben, don't," but he'd already lurched away, scrambling out from behind the headstone and bolting for the trees to the north of them.

Sorcha closed her eyes tightly and hunkered down behind the tombstone. She pressed her forehead to her knees and crossed her cold fingers, muttering, "Run, run, run…Oh, my God, Ben, run."

The next gunshot rang out with a 'Crack!' that made her whole body jerk. She opened her eyes and stared at her knees as the shot echoed ominously. She felt like a coward hiding like this and desperately wanted to peek around the stone, but if she did, whoever was out there might see her and then Ben's gambit would be a sure loss. She consoled herself with the thought that he was *her* Ben, and Enid had yet to tell anyone in her world about him, which meant he couldn't die now. He just couldn't.

She waited for what felt like an eternity but was probably only ten minutes or so. Her breath came shallowly, and she tried to listen past the pounding of her heart for any sign that Ben wasn't, even now, lying dead just beyond the graveyard.

What was left of the afternoon light was fading fast when she heard cautious footfalls. She looked frantically around the near vicinity for a rock to throw or something suitable to defend herself with, but Ben's voice came softly, "Sorcha!"

She let out a cry of relief and sprang up, but after crouching for so long on the cold ground, her legs failed her after two wobbly steps, and she sprawled forward into Ben's arms.

"Who was it? Did you see him?" Her feet began to tingle as the circulation returned.

"No. He got away." Ben was breathing hard. "Can you walk?"

"Yeah." They started back to the house. She looked over at the oak grove and gasped when she saw the dark silhouette of a man walking towards them in the gloom of the twilight.

"It's Skip," Ben said. "He heard the shots."

The sound of sirens faded in and out on the cold air. "If Skip heard them, then Grammy Fay did, too," she said.

She couldn't see the house from here, but a flicker of light through the trees and a faint cry of, "Sorcha!" told her Fay was concerned and out looking for her with a flashlight. She would head straight for the graveyard.

They intercepted Skip's path and he joined them on the walk to the house. "Now, Sorcha," he said, "I don't want to tell you what to do, but I think you know how difficult it's going to be to explain this to the cops."

"I wasn't planning on telling them anything," she replied. "I've spent my whole life avoiding the loony bin. You think I'm going to blow it now just because someone wants me dead?" Her voice was tinged with irony.

Ben looked over at the older man. "Did you find any clues?"

Skip lifted his hand. Pinched between finger and thumb was a bullet casing. ".22 long range cartridge. From those trees, with that rifle, he was too far away for an accurate shot. Not a hunter, or at least not a good one."

Sorcha silently thanked her lucky stars her would-be assassin wasn't a pro. She could barely make out Fay in the distance now and raised her hand. "I'm okay, Grammy!" she yelled.

"You find anything?" Skip asked.

"Fast runner. Prints were size ten Nike's."

"Really?" Sorcha asked. "You could tell that?"

"Yeah, Sorch, all Native Americans can read tracks," Ben said. "Especially when the print is the same size as mine and there's a logo stamped in the dirt."

She socked him on the arm and then noticed he was still wearing her hat and scarf. The girly cashmere checked knit contrasted sharply with his masculinity. It looked absurd, and she giggled. She saw the whiteness of his teeth against the shadowy backdrop of his face as he grinned back. He put one hand behind his head and stopped walking long enough to pose for her.

"You like this look on me?" Rather than make him look feminine, the stance demonstrated to Sorcha how confident he was with his sexuality.

It struck her as hysterically funny, though, and suddenly she couldn't stop laughing long enough to respond, realizing even as she doubled over from abdominal spasms that this was a reaction to the shock and fear of having been shot at. Vaguely, she heard Skip say, "Now look what you did," but she was too caught up in uncontrolled mirth.

It took her awhile to restrain herself, and it didn't help when she glanced over and saw that Ben had pushed the hat to one side at a jaunty angle.

"Take that damned thing off!" Skip said, and Ben complied, but he responded, "Give the girl a break. She needs to let off some steam."

Back at the house, Fay fussed over them. "I'm so glad you were here, Mr. Webster. We've had hunters stray onto our land before, but never so close to the house."

"Call me Skip. It was just lucky I came by early to pick Ben up. Whoever it was is long gone, though."

The police officer who showed up seemed bored and got more so as Skip, Ben and Sorcha downplayed the facts. There was no mention of the shots coming close to actually hitting anyone. Officer Hurley took their statements and said, "We'll keep an eye out."

Fay took exception to his blasé handling of the situation. "Young man, I'll have you know our property is both fenced and posted with private property signs. Whoever did this had to have knowingly entered."

"Yes, ma'am, I'll make a note of that, but since this was the intruder's first offense, it's possible he was just following injured game onto your land."

"And he had to shoot at it three times?" Fay said indignantly.

"Or maybe it was just some kids out being stupid," Skip said. "No harm done."

He rested his hand lightly on Fay's arm and Sorcha saw her look down at it and then back up to Skip's face. He was around her age and not unattractive, with his longish seventies-style shag haircut and the same slightly hooked aquiline nose all the Webster men seemed to have. He had far less natural charm than Ben, but Fay was mollified nonetheless.

"Alright," she said grudgingly. "I suppose there's nothing you can do, but really, there should be an intelligence test or something before giving out hunting licenses."

The officer shot Skip a grateful look and left with a parting, "Call right away if he comes back."

Fay started to close the door, but Skip said, "I'm afraid Ben and I can't stay."

"Oh, that's too bad," Fay said. Sorcha winced at the almost simpering look on her grandmother's face. Fay was long out of practice when it came to flirting, but it looked like Skip had inspired her to try. He wasn't blind to it, either, from the gleam in his blue eyes.

Sorcha felt Ben come up close behind her. Softly, he said, "And love is in the air."

She elbowed him in the stomach and was rewarded with a satisfying, "Oof!"

He didn't try to kiss her this time when he left, and she couldn't decide whether she was grateful or disappointed. On the one hand, she could do without a PDA in front of her grandmother and Skip, but on the other hand…she wished she and Ben could be alone.

In bed, she lay awake thinking about who wanted her dead and why. Two hundred years ago, the Webster family had put into motion an entire society dedicated to protecting her, so it stood to reason that whoever wanted to harm her also had roots back to Enid. Given the insignificance of

99

Enid's life thus far, Sorcha couldn't imagine what she could have possibly said or done to bring this down upon her. And why on earth had the Webster family gotten involved in the first place? Sorcha knew it was pointless to think about it, but the same stubbornness that had spurred her to search for Enid's date of death was sending her thoughts spinning now.

As she finally began to doze, those thoughts drifted to Ben and his selfless act of courage; how he'd lured the gunman's fire and then chased him away, probably saving her life. It wasn't the first time it occurred to her that there was more to Ben than good looks and sarcasm.

Chapter Sixteen

Enid

Upon waking, Enid found herself under her mother's scrutiny again. Bluebird held up the remains of the dress Enid had cut apart the day before. She'd taken care to hide the scraps beneath her sleeping furs, but it appeared Bluebird had discovered them while she slept.

"Why have you done this, and where is the rest of the cloth?"

Enid had no ready lie at hand, so she winged it. "I – I pulled it apart to make a blanket." She looked around her, as if the fabric in question should be nearby.

Bluebird's face froze into an affronted mask. "Do you suggest that it has been stolen? Here among those who have given you food and shelter?"

Confronted by her mother's illogic, Enid felt as if the world tilted just slightly on its axis. Bluebird had kidnapped her but could not see her actions for what they were. For all her mother knew, Enid could have been happy with her father. It took a monumental effort not to lash out at her. While Sorcha could allow the bonds of self-control to stretch once in a while, Enid could not afford to, not here.

"Perhaps I dropped it on the way to the latrine," she said.

Bluebird looked skeptical but seemed willing to let it slide. "Spotted Fawn has gone with Walks Like a Moose's sister. You need to prepare for your meeting with the medicine man. I will allow you to wear my finest robe. When the sun is higher, we will bathe. Until then, you will make yourself useful."

Enid was introduced to the 'sisters' her mother had mentioned, three round-faced women whose resemblance to each other was so strong they must be real sisters. The tallest of the three carried an infant in a cradleboard on her back and looked at Bluebird with an undisguised enmity that Enid's mother didn't seem to notice. All three women spoke a smattering of English, and as they instructed Enid in preparing squash for baking, it became rapidly clear that although her mother had been adopted into the clan, she had not been accepted by all. Perhaps it was the laconic way she helped with the chore at hand, producing far less than the others. Or maybe it was her attitude, an unsubtle superiority that possibly stemmed from the knowledge that she was more attractive than her sisters.

Oddly, the dynamic between these women and her mother reminded Enid of Kristin Barber and her clique. Bluebird was the interloper, but she'd either gained or taken some advantage that put her in a position of leadership.

After the squashes had been tucked carefully around most of the banked fires in the longhouse, Enid was hustled outside by her mother. For Joseph's sake, she was glad the weather had drastically changed, and the small amount of snow that had fallen yesterday had all but melted. A group of young men were playing a rowdy game of lacrosse on a flat dirt lot adjoining the corn field. They stopped to stare at Enid as Bluebird marched her past.

Everyone seemed to be taking advantage of the warm morning sun. The shore of the bathing spot was teeming with children. Mothers stripped them naked and herded them into the frigid water two or three at a time. Enid saw a girl of maybe three refuse to step into the water. She clung to her mother until the woman peeled her little fingers away from her skirt and set her into the river up to her thighs. The child didn't cry out until a slightly older boy who was already in the water splashed her – then her shrill scream startled some nearby birds from the trees.

Bluebird stripped down and washed, too, this time. Enid kept her underclothes on again, ignoring the snickers of the other bathers.

On the way back to the longhouse, a flash of pale lavender caught her eye; the dried-up petals of several late-blooming flowers protruding from a low plant. She stopped and quickly reached down to grasp a handful of the plant's wilted leaves. It was Bee Balm, which would make a good antiseptic rinse for Joseph. She shoved the leaves into her left sleeve, for lack of a better place to put them.

Her mother plaited Enid's hair and then turned her back so Enid could return the favor. Bluebird had said she would allow Enid to wear her best robe, but the soft deerskin tunic she was given was plain in comparison to the beaded dress Bluebird wore over her skirt and leggings.

This time when they walked through the village, Bluebird strolled importantly along with her chin raised. Enid sent several longing glances in the direction of the latrine, which she couldn't see over the palisade. Would Joseph manage to remain hidden and safe? Would she ever have a moment to herself to sneak food to him? It seemed unlikely today.

102

The medicine man lived separately from his clan in a domed wigwam about a hundred yards upstream of the bathing spot. From the way her mother was acting, Enid expected him to be an imposing figure, and that assumption proved correct. The man in the brightly decorated robes who swept the curtained door aside and stood on the wigwam's threshold was of average height and build, but his unpleasant countenance oozed arrogant disdain. Unlike Bluebird's arrogance, it was not gained from knowing he was attractive. His hair was singed on the sides in a Mohawk, but he had a small, pinched nose that reminded her of a woman's nose job gone wrong in Sorcha's world. His eyes bulged out alarmingly and his lips were thin in a wide mouth. Overall, the Haudenosaunee medicine man looked like a fish, albeit a royal one. Enid was immediately wary of him, even though he politely held the door skin aside so they could enter.

Walks Like a Moose was already there, sitting on a fur near the medicine man's fire. The wigwam was roomier than she'd expected, but dark and smoky with a bitter burnt-hair smell. As her eyes adjusted, she saw that the walls were covered with bundles of dried tobacco and herbs, with the occasional mask or dried gourd hung from the curved poles that supported the bark walls. Enid blinked in surprise at a European-style bed and chest against the far wall. Atop the chest sat an unlit oil lamp, an inkwell and some loose papers.

She'd expected Bluebird to have to translate, but the medicine man said, "I am James Butler."

Enid produced an awkward curtsey. "Enid Thompson."

"Your mother tells me you were born with two spirits. I have met such people in my travels across the ocean to the white man's homeland. They are born as men, but have a second spirit within, a female one that confuses them. Tell me, is this the case with your second spirit?"

Before Enid could open her mouth to deny it, Bluebird said, "Enid does not have a second spirit, but one spirit split in two. The other half of her spirit lives in the future."

James Butler's eyelids flickered in a way that suggested he already knew this. Walks Like a Moose would have told him everything Bluebird had revealed about her daughter. "Let the girl speak."

Enid was nervous but prepared. "My spirit is whole and lives only within me. My mother remembers the young girl who loved to tell tales."

Bluebird gasped in indignation, but James Butler smiled. It wasn't a pleasant look for him; he resembled a boy about to squish a bug and then poke at its guts with a stick.

"I have learned much on my journeys and brought that knowledge home to my people. There grows a wild plant in these hills that we have found many uses for over the centuries. Its Latin name is *Cannabis sativa* and when smoked, it can coerce an unwilling person to be truthful."

Enid didn't react. Sorcha and her friends had never smoked pot, but she'd heard it referred to by a number of names, including cannabis. From what she'd been told, there was a very good chance the weed would get her to talk, and quite volubly, but she didn't allow her concern to show on her face.

Bluebird said, "Give it to her."

Enid met her mother's eyes, which were glittering with hostility. James Butler made a move towards the back of the wigwam, but shouts from outside pulled his attention away from his goal.

Over the sound of several voices raised in panic, a woman's screams could be heard. Enid didn't understand the words, but the others did. Walks Like a Moose scrambled to his feet as the medicine man grabbed a mask from the wall, strode swiftly to the door flap and ducked outside. Enid followed as her mother and stepfather went out to see what the commotion was. A dozen or so people flanked a woman who was running up the path, screaming, with a limp child in her arms. James Butler, now wearing the mask, rushed to meet her and took the child. He barked a command, and someone removed their robe and dropped it to the ground so he could place the child upon it.

From where she stood, Enid couldn't tell if the unconscious child was a girl or a boy. After a brief moment examining the child, the medicine man straightened up and bellowed, "Enid Thompson!"

It was the last thing Enid expected, to be suddenly singled out in the middle of what was obviously a great tragedy for the tribe. Did he blame her for this? Would he tell them her arrival caused it?

He stood and turned toward her as Walks Like a Moose grasped her upper arms from behind and forced her forward. She saw the child, a naked girl with blue-tinged lips. Her sparse black hair clung wetly to her skull.

Drowned.

The medicine man spoke in his native tongue from behind the distorted, grimacing red face of the mask. His voice was somehow magnified, the cadence and volume of his words increasing at the end of his proclamation. Then he pointed at Enid and translated what he'd said to the onlookers. "The Great Spirit sent me a vision. If you spoke truth and your spirit is whole, the child will die."

Enid inhaled sharply, but otherwise didn't hesitate. She dropped to her hands and knees and gently tilted the girl's head back. There was no need to listen for breath sounds because it was obvious there weren't any, but she held her fingers to the girl's neck, hoping for a pulse. When nothing fluttered there, she ran her fingers down the girl's chest until she found the breastbone, then clasped her hands, locked her elbows and began compressions. After 30 quick thrusts, she placed her mouth over the child's and forced two breaths into her lungs. The girl's slack, cold lips felt nothing like the plastic mouth of the dummy Sorcha had practiced on in Health Class.

As she kept at it, she vaguely heard the mother's subdued sobs and the murmurs of the crowd. She tried to remember how long she should keep the CPR up before conceding death. If the child had been submersed for too long, nothing she did would bring her back. The murmurs were becoming grumbles as the people watching saw no improvement.

"One, two, three, four…" Enid hadn't realized she'd begun counting aloud. Her breath was coming faster now with the unaccustomed exertion and her thighs burned from supporting the weight of her torso. Just when she began to think it had all been in vain, that the child would die and Enid would be torn apart by those watching her fail the medicine man's challenge, the girl's eyes opened, and she began to cough. Then she spasmodically pulled her knees to her chest, rolled to her side and vomited a copious amount of water onto the ground.

The crowd, which had grown considerably while she worked, shouted its approval. Enid found herself nudged roughly aside by the girl's mother, who pulled the coughing and choking child into her arms. Helping hands wrapped the hypothermic girl in robes.

Stiffly, Enid stood and stared at the ground. Whether James Butler had truly had a vision or had merely guessed that Enid's knowledge of future things could save the child was irrelevant. He'd given her an impossible choice, and he'd done it to force her hand. She knew what she would see in his eyes when she gathered enough courage to look, and she was right. He'd removed the mask, and his face was suffused with triumph, but in addition, the medicine man looked at her with something bordering on admiration. When he ran his gaze down her body and back up again, she felt her skin crawl.

If she thought she would be thanked, she was mistaken. The mother of the girl spoke a few grateful words to James Butler and then she and the rest of the crowd walked back down the path. It was as if Enid was invisible.

James Butler narrowed his eyes at her. "You expected thanks, but she sees you as the tool I used to save her daughter."

"Is that what I am to become? A tool?" Enid flashed on the derogatory slang meaning of tool in Sorcha's world, and certainly felt like one.

"All people are tools to be used as the Creator sees fit."

He walked past Bluebird and Walks Like a Moose on the way to his wigwam. "I accept Enid Thompson as my apprentice. We begin on the morrow."

Back at the longhouse, Bluebird made Enid change into the outfit she'd worn the day before, and the rest of the afternoon was spent pounding dried corn into flour. After that, the tribe held an impromptu celebration in the main clearing. A hunting party had brought down a large buck the day before, and it had been roasting on a spit all day. Torches were lit when the sun went down. The family of the near-drowned child presented James Butler with corn mash and tobacco. He and a group of men and women wearing masks similar to his danced and chanted and shook rattles.

Now that Enid had been given the honor of becoming the medicine man's apprentice, Bluebird had reverted to the caring mother she'd been that first day. She was so falsely solicitous, in fact, that Enid felt smothered. At the first opportunity, she faded as far back from the merriment as she could, finally finding the right moment to make a break for the latrine.

The moon was a mere fingernail in the sky, making the trek a dark and spooky one. The wind was calm, and a low fog had begun to form. When a young man and woman who'd apparently snuck away to be alone together came out of nowhere, she shrieked in fright. They laughed and the woman said something in her language, but Enid hurried on. In the near blackness, it took her some time to locate Joseph's hiding spot, but she was confident that if she could hardly see ten feet in front of her, then no one would be able to see her.

Just outside the hemlock thicket, she whispered, "Joseph!"

For a moment she feared he'd gone or had been discovered or – it was too painful to contemplate what else might have happened – but he made a sound like, "Uh."

She crawled inside. It was pitch black. Enid felt his hands fumble for her until he found her shoulders. He couldn't very well ask her anything, so she began to talk quietly.

"I brought you some food. Baked squash, very soft." She reached inside her robes and untied her pocket. His hands slid down her arms and she managed to pass the squash to him. To mask the sounds he made trying to eat it, she continued talking.

"The other half of my spirit lives in a time of great knowledge. I have learned that once your injury heals, you will be able to train yourself to speak again. You do not have to be mute. Can you write?"

He said, "Mm," and she immediately apologized. "I will try not to ask questions."

106

He found her hand and drew his finger along her palm repeatedly until she asked, "Is that a 'y' for 'yes?'"

He said, "Mm," and then wrote the 'y' again.

"Let me feel an 'n' for 'no,'" she said.

He made the 'n.'

"So the answer to my question is yes, you can write. I wish it were light so you could write in the dirt and we could talk. I was not free to come until now, but I was able to sneak away because the whole village is celebrating. Can you hear it? If it does not hurt to make sounds, you could say one 'mm' for yes and two for no."

He said, "Mm."

"Are you finished with the squash? It was as much as I could hide. Did you also finish the tea I made you? I brought a handful of bee balm leaves but did not have a chance to steep it. I hope you filled the pot with snow before it melted-"

His hand found her mouth and he pinched her lips together with his fingers. She laughed, but with her mouth shut, it forced an indelicate snort out her nose. He released her lips and cupped her cheek briefly before sliding his fingers into her hair. His other hand found the small of her back and urged her closer. He didn't try to kiss her this time, just pulled her into his arms and held her.

Chapter Seventeen

Sorcha

Grammy Fay was excited about Halloween, or as she liked to call it, 'Samhain.' She'd draped the front porch with fake spider webs and put out decorations. Every year Sorcha wondered why she went to all the trouble when no one ever came trick-or-treating this far from town. Even the families in the duplexes at the end of the lane left the area to mine the newer housing developments for candy.

"I got a new witch at the drugstore," Fay said at the breakfast table. "It has a sensor that tells it when someone is walking by, and it cackles."

"Sounds very spooky."

Sorcha had wanted to skip breakfast so she could surf the Internet for information on Sarah, but Fay had made her special pumpkin pancakes, so Sorcha dutifully sat and ate. Her comment on the new witch must have sounded less than enthusiastic, because Fay put her hands on her hips and asked, "Everything okay? Can we talk about Enid yet?"

Sorcha shook her head. "I'd rather not. There's a lot going on right now. Everything feels so…unstable."

"That's because the barrier between us and the spirit world is thinnest this time of year. You of all people would be sensitive to that."

Sorcha responded to her grandmother's whimsy with a non-committal, "Hm," and glanced at the clock over the stove. She took a few more minutes to wolf down the last of the pancakes before thanking Fay and dashing up to her bedroom. She opened the old trunk at the foot of her bed and dug out the genealogy research binder she'd put together over the years. Some time ago, she'd made a tissue paper charcoal rub of the words inscribed on Sarah's headstone. She took the fragile, folded paper out of the folder and tucked it into her backpack.

The sky was overcast with the kind of solid cloud cover that had no form to it but was simply a blanket of greyish white stretching to the horizon. It was starting to get darker in the mornings as the days got shorter. Sorcha stepped over the roots of the old oak tree and headed for Paula's car, her breath condensing in the crisp air.

She was used to seeing Luanne, but the passenger in the back seat this morning was not Ben.

"Hello, Sunshine," John said as Sorcha got in and sat. "Look who's been assigned to keep you safe today."

Paula's eyes in the rearview mirror told Sorcha exactly what her opinion of John's presence was. Sorcha reached for her seat belt, disturbed that she had to nudge John's thigh aside to get to the buckle. He smelled like cigarette smoke.

Luanne got right to it. "What happened with Enid yesterday?"

"Not much," Sorcha said. "The village medicine man made her his apprentice. Maybe not a career choice she would have chosen if anyone had bothered to ask, but hey, that's life in the eighteenth century."

Her poor attempt at a joke seemed to roll right over Luanne, who had a tense look about her that made Sorcha say, "It might help if I knew what you were waiting to hear."

John opened his mouth to respond, but Luanne jabbed a finger in his direction and snapped, "Don't!"

Sorcha saw Paula's eyebrows rise in the rearview mirror. Luanne had no love for her cousin, that much was apparent.

"I was just going to say that we couldn't tell her anything," John replied. "Isn't that what the elders want? To keep her in the dark?"

"Shut it, you little cretin," Luanne said in a low voice.

"Or what?" John asked. "It doesn't matter what I say. The past has already happened."

Luanne turned to Sorcha. "I'm sorry for this. Not all of us agree on how this should be handled. There are a few, very much in the minority," she narrowed her eyes at John, "who want to take a more proactive stance."

"Proactive?" Sorcha asked. "Like how?"

John laughed. "Like telling you what you need to do to make sure you actually do it, instead of hoping things work out."

Luanne pounced. "Like things already have? Pick one or the other, John. Has the past already happened, or should we influence it to happen?"

"I'm getting a headache," Paula muttered.

Sorcha unzipped her backpack, pulled out the charcoal rub and passed it over to Luanne. "Ben said you might be able to find out what this says."

Luanne unfolded the paper and said, "Oh, wow. Where'd you get this?"

"It's from our cemetery. One of the gravestones."

"You have a cemetery? On your land?" She sounded beyond envious.

"Yeah. I've identified all the occupants, except Sarah there."

Luanne studied the letters the charcoal revealed. "I can't read it, but I think I know someone who can."

"Harry the Hobo?" Sorcha asked.

John snorted, but Luanne said, "Don't call him that. He's my uncle. He used to run the old Native American Artifacts Museum."

"Yeah, until he went nuts," John said.

"He's not nuts. He's a brilliant man."

"I remember him," Paula said. "On that field trip, remember Sorch? When the horse fell over and you were all covered in sawdust? He was funny. The man, not the horse."

Sorcha did remember. The museum curator wore traditional Iroquois garb and had long dark hair pulled back into one thick braid. He'd seemed fierce and kind at the same time, gently brushing the sawdust off Sorcha's legs and telling her tongue-in-cheek that she was covered in history. That man hardly resembled the scruffy, unsociable old man who'd watched the WPS meeting from the shadows of the trees.

"What happened to him?" she asked.

"He and my dad were twins," Luanne said. "When dad died, Harry just kind of retreated from the world."

Paula glanced over. "So, Skip, Sarge and Harry the Hobo are all your uncles? What's with the nicknames?"

"You really wanna know?" John asked. His grin was devilish.

Luanne shifted abruptly in her seat like she was going to lunge at him. "Shut your face."

"What?" John shrugged innocently. "I'm not going to say anything about their first names all being Ben."

Luanne turned to Paula and said through clenched teeth, "Pull over."

Paula didn't have to be told twice. She hit the brakes hard enough to make the small car's wheels screech on the highway asphalt. They came to a stop on the shoulder several hundred yards from the exit to town.

"Get out," Luanne said.

"Really?" John said. "That's kind of harsh, isn't it? Skip said I was supposed to watch her."

Luanne glared at him. "You think I don't know what you did to Ben?"

"Which Ben?" John muttered, but Luanne ignored him and continued.

"We all know. Everyone in the family thinks you're a complete jerk. No one trusts you; no one likes you. Ben didn't say anything about you jumping him because he feels sorry for you, but I don't. Get out."

John's face had retained a look of boredom until that last bit, and then his cheeks grew dark and his chin dropped to his chest. Sorcha leaned against the car door as far away as she could get, fully expecting him to go ballistic, but all he did was tell her coolly, "You wouldn't want him if you knew what he was capable of."

He got out and slammed the door. Paula immediately gunned it and left him standing there.

It was only a short drive to Luanne's bus stop from there. Sorcha's mind was reeling. Why were all the Webster men named Ben? Ben had let it slip once, that day he'd said "all the Bens do," but then he'd distracted her by telling her about John's dad – how Sarge had paid so much attention to Ben after his dad died, and how jealous John had been. And now Luanne was saying Ben felt sorry for John, which didn't add up.

Luanne got out, leaned in, and said, "I know you're confused, but believe me when I say there's a lot at stake here. Don't listen to John. Ben genuinely cares for you."

She walked away and Paula pulled back onto the road. "Dang. That was intense."

"I know, huh?"

"Why name all four brothers Ben?"

Sorcha thought about it for a moment. "Enid probably says something about someone named Ben. I think they got all their information from things she said in the past. I just don't know who she said it to."

"Do you think John's right? That they should just tell you what you should do?"

"I wish I knew what to believe." Sorcha stared out the window at the landscape rushing by. She thought about being in Joseph's arms and compared it to being held by Ben. The only thing that felt the same between the two was the sense that despite the strong arms around her, she wasn't safe.

Ben was waiting in the parking lot. Sorcha didn't need to see his face to know how he felt about John usurping his spot in Paula's car. As soon as Sorcha got out, he took her arm and steered her toward the school.

"Where's John?" he asked.

Paula responded, "He got his ass hat handed to him by Luanne."

Ben's stiff face immediately softened, and he chuckled. "Loony's reliable that way."

111

A car was coming down the dirt aisle toward them, faster than it should. It came to a stop and Sorcha was not surprised to see John get out. He said, "Thanks for the ride, man," to the driver, who then drove away.

Ben's hand tightened on Sorcha's arm as John loped up and took her other arm, shooting Ben a challenging look. "You wanna pull and see who gets the biggest chunk of her?"

Sorcha yanked her arm away from John and clung to Ben. "I'm not a wishbone."

John smirked at her. "You sure about that?"

Ben looked at John with contempt. "Guess who I just talked to?"

"Is this a multiple-choice question?"

"Principal Kessler," Ben said. "You didn't have detention yesterday."

"So? The protection detail is stupid. I already showed you how easy it was to sneak past them."

"Exactly my point. If you did it once, you could do it again." Ben nodded down at John's feet. "What size are those Nikes?"

"You got a foot fetish, Coz?"

"Nah, they just look about the same size as mine."

"Well, I'm not about to lend them to you, so you can get that outta your head right now."

"Enough!" Sorcha said, voice raised. She glared at John. "Were you or were you not the one who tried to kill me yesterday?"

"What?" Paula said.

John threw his head back and laughed heartily, but Sorcha could tell it was forced.

"I wasn't trying to kill you – just shake things up a little."

"What does that mean?" she asked.

"You poor, stupid kid. You still have no idea what they want you to do. What they need you to do."

"John." Ben's upper lip curled under, baring his gritted teeth.

"Yeah, you can kick my ass, Benjamin, or try to, but not before I tell her. You don't think she deserves to know exactly what she's sacrificing so you and all the other Bens can be *born*?"

"You, too, *Benjamin John Nelson*," Ben snapped. "You think somehow you'd be the only one to survive?"

John made a 'tch' sound. "Aren't you forgetting something? You're the one who told me Sarge wasn't my real dad, remember? When you kicked the crap out of me and spent two years in juvie for it? But, yeah, you were right. I had a paternity test done. Saved up my allowance for a whole year and bought it off the internet. I'm not a Ben after all."

112

"That's not true," Ben said.

"Oh, but it is, Coz. And I won't cry when you're gone."

"You'd kill us all?"

"Is that what it would be? Because I don't think there'll be any bodies lying around. No bodies, no birth certificates, nothing." He leaned forward and said viciously, "Even I won't remember you."

"Okay." Ben lifted his hands. "Except that someone had to be your father, and I happen to know who that someone was. Want a clue?" Ben leaned forward and said in the same vicious tone John had just used, "His name was *Ben*."

"Bull." But John didn't sound so sure of himself all of a sudden.

Ben uttered a short, humorless laugh. "That paternity test wasn't a hundred percent match to Sarge, but it didn't completely exclude him, did it? That's because Sarge is biologically related to you. If you knew who your dad really was, we wouldn't be having this discussion. You'd know you were my cousin – *by blood* – and you'd do anything in your power to make sure Enid—"

He stopped and looked at Sorcha's appalled face.

"Enid what?" she asked.

Ben's mouth fell open and he shook his head minutely. In a tortured whisper, he said, "I can't tell you."

But she knew. It was finally clear to her why this entire family had set up such an elaborate scheme to ensure that what had already happened, did indeed happen.

Through motionless lips, she uttered, "I die, don't I?"

John laughed again and this time his amusement was genuine. "Ho, I didn't even have to spill the beans."

"Shut *up!*" Ben threw a swift punch that connected with John's face in a meaty-sounding crunch. Blood spurted from John's nostrils. He bent over and cupped his hands around his nose, groaning and stamping one foot in pain.

Sorcha let go of Ben's arm and took several steps back, staring at him, betrayal twisting her insides.

Paula put an arm around her shoulders and said in a high-pitched voice, "Is it true? Does Enid die?"

Before Ben could respond, someone shouted, "Hey!"

Sorcha stared at Ben, only peripherally aware as Dalton and two of his friends ran up. They positioned themselves protectively between John and the girls. Dalton said to Ben, "Everything okay here? Need any assistance, bro?"

Ben was staring back at Sorcha, shaking his head slowly.

Paula took charge. "Thanks Dalton. You came in the nick of time. These two morons were just saying goodbye to me and Sorch. Will you walk us to class?"

"Be glad to," Dalton said.

Once Sorcha broke off eye contact with Ben, she lost track of time. She walked into school, got her History book out of her locker and went to class, all without much conscious thought. It wasn't until she was supposed to be listening to Mr. Lee lecturing about the aftermath of the Civil War that it occurred to her that Enid wasn't just supposed to die, but that she already had – and that it would be soon.

Without a word, she stood and walked out of the classroom, deaf to Mr. Lee's, "Miss Sloane? Are you alright?"

She walked toward the nearest building exit, every step sending a little squeak echoing down the empty corridor. Outside, she passed the flagpole and the bus stop and just kept walking. She trudged along as her mind sifted through the events of the last week, examining evidence and either filing it away or discarding it.

The most important thing, the fact of Enid's death, haunted her. She'd always hoped they would live to be old biddies and die together in their sleep. Everyone wished to die painlessly, much loved and missed by someone. If Enid's half of her soul was as essential as she suspected it was, death would claim them at the exact same moment. She'd always believed Enid was her ancestor, but since Enid was about to die without children, Sorcha would have never been born if that were true.

She thought of Sarah then. Jedediah's little girl could very well have been the ancestor she'd been searching for all along. She'd been so focused on finding Enid's date of death, and now she could only be grateful that she never had. Like Grammy Fay had always told her, sometimes it's better not to know.

By the time she reached the path along the road that led to Bear Talker's stone, Ben had come alongside her on his bike and begun walking with her. She didn't ignore him, but didn't acknowledge him either, just kept moving forward one step at a time.

Among the trees, the grey day got darker. She stopped in the center of the circle and her gaze drifted up to the tops of the pines. They whispered softly in the mild breeze. She imagined she could almost feel the separation between the spirit world and this one. Fay had said the barrier was thin this time of year, and at that moment, Sorcha felt it was as fragile as the tissue paper charcoal rub of the mysterious words on Sarah's gravestone.

"Will it happen tomorrow?" she asked.

From somewhere behind her, close, Ben replied, "We think so."

"How do I die?"

"Sorcha." He put a hand on her shoulder. She shrugged it off, but not angrily. She was in the grip of a kind of trance and didn't want to snap out of it. To do so would expose her to the pain and sorrow that was waiting for her.

"Tell me. So I know what I need to do."

"Will you do it?"

She turned to him then. His eyes, so like Joseph's, shone with unshed tears.

"Joseph is your ancestor, isn't he?" she asked.

Ben nodded, the movement dislodging a lone tear, which slid down one cheek.

"They catch him, don't they? At the Haudenosaunee village?"

Another nod.

"And Enid saves him?"

Ben's head drifted to the side and his mouth compressed into a thin, sad line. His eyes begged her to understand. He wiped his cheek and said in a thick voice, "Yes."

"And if she doesn't, you won't be born. The entire Webster family will never have existed. That's what John meant."

He reached for her again and she let him pull her into his arms, releasing a deep sigh into the crook of his neck.

"Please don't hate me," he said quietly.

She pulled back and looked into his eyes. "Will you tell me now? About Joseph and what I need to tell him?"

He took her hand and pulled her toward his bike. "I'll show you."

She rode in front of him on the handlebars all the way to Luanne's bus stop. They only had to wait a few minutes before the bus arrived. Ben waved to the driver and pushed his bike off the curb in front of the bus. He pulled down an aluminum rack and lifted the bike onto it like he did it all the time.

In the warm bus, she sat very close to him, leaning against his shoulder. He held her hand between both of his in his lap.

"Will you get in trouble for telling me?"

His mouth twisted in a rueful grimace. "Maybe it's supposed to happen this way."

"A paradox wrapped in a conundrum."

"With a bow on top."

She laughed a little, but mostly for his benefit.

The bus dropped them on the sidewalk directly across from their destination, Green Plains Community College. He chained his bike to a rack and led her to a wing that looked newer than the main building. The plaque over the glass doors read, "WPS Native American Studies."

Sorcha stopped and squinted at the words. "Oh, I get it now. Webster Protection Society."

Ben said, "Mystery solved."

"Luanne mentioned your uncle Harry donated all the items from the old Native American Artifacts Museum to her school, but…an entire wing? If he could afford that, why is he homeless now?"

Ben opened the door for her, and she entered the warm lobby. "Because he didn't pay for the wing, the Society did. Uncle Harry ran the museum for all those years looking for you."

He took her hand and led her down a wide hallway hung with Native American-themed paintings. At the end was a large room lit with skylights and filled with display cases. There were no other people present, just a mannequin of a Native American brave sitting on a large stuffed horse. The horse was decked out in a woven blanket and braided tack and stood on a raised dais at the very center of the room.

Despite her mood, she laughed. "Look! There's the horse that tried to kill me."

Ben gave her a funny look and she said, "I'll tell you all about it someday."

He held her gaze. "I'll hold you to that."

She smiled and glanced around at the artifacts on display. "So how did Uncle Harry expect to find me?"

"He looked at every little girl that came through on field trips. We didn't know you and Enid were nothing alike. He was looking for her." He pointed.

On the wall, in a glass-fronted frame, hung a small portrait of Enid. Sorcha walked over and stood looking up at it in wonder. It was a charcoal sketch done on paper and appeared to be very fragile.

"Joseph did this, didn't he?"

"Yeah."

She studied the confident strokes and subtle shading for a moment before saying, "It looks like her. He was talented. I had no idea."

"Um…there's one more thing I wanted you to see, but it's locked up. I was thinking, maybe if we called Loony and told her we were here, she could get out of class and come show it to you."

"She's going to be pissed, though, right? Except, it was John who made me realize…"

Ben took out his cell phone and raised his eyebrows. "Oh, definitely, she's gonna rip me a new one, but I don't care about that anymore."

After he called his sister, it took her about three minutes to storm into the room.

"You have *got* to be kidding me!" Luanne's voice was just short of a shout.

"It's not his fault," Sorcha said. "Blame John."

Luanne looked very much as if her head was about to explode. "I. Will. Kill. Him."

"And I'll load the gun for you," Ben said. "But first, can Sorcha see Joseph's will?"

"*What?*" Luanne's voice was in the range that only dogs could hear.

"Chill, okay?" Ben snapped. "She knows. Just about everything. We owe it to her to be honest now."

Luanne's head went back, and she blinked a few times. She took a deep breath and let it out in a long sigh. "Fine. I guess it's too late now."

She spun on her heel and stalked back down the hallway. A few minutes later, she reappeared with a leather binder. She set it on one of the display cases and opened it. "Be careful."

Sorcha looked down at the first page, which was encased in protective clear plastic. It was hand-written in ink in formal eighteenth century style.

"I, Joseph M. Webster, do make and declare this instrument, written in my own Hand, to be my sole Will and Testament.

"To my Wife, Spotted Fawn…"

Sorcha closed her eyes against the burn of sudden tears. So Joseph married Enid's half-sister. Sorcha glanced over at Ben. Technically, he was distantly related to Enid.

"Keep reading," Ben urged.

Sorcha began again.

"To my Wife, Spotted Fawn, I bequeath the use and benefit of my estate in its entirety, all household furniture and linens, for the term of her natural life. Upon her decease, the estate shall pass to my remaining child, my heir and Beloved Son, Benjamin.

"To Benjamin, I leave written testament of that which must be Documented for Posterity.

"In my youth, I was victimized most grievously by a band of Mohawk warriors, wherein I suffered the loss of my tongue. This injury was inflicted with the intention of Silencing me forever in regards to what follows. My good Wife had a sister whose name was Enid, and I was acquainted with this sister before my Wife was full grown. Enid was known by the Haudenosaunee people to be a Witch with two souls, and I cannot argue the fact for my own Uncle, Bear Talker, a Respected Medicine Man, attended her birth and Proclaimed it. One half of her soul resided in Enid; another in a future Self. Her knowledge of the Future was passed on to me in no small part on the date of her death, and in order to fulfill the prophecies Enid laid before me, it is henceforth my Destiny to ensure her words pass to my Progeny. With no desire to cause hurt to my Wife after her many years of devoted Marriage, I must declare I held Enid in Highest Regard and Respect, for she was my first Love. If not for the ultimate sacrifice of her Life, I would have been killed at the behest of the elders of Haudenosaunee village which later adopted me. Although she bade me accept this sacrifice because it was Preordained, I bear great Shame for her Death, which she gave to me in ignorance of whether her future soul would Live on. Therefore all who follow me should Heed, in perpetuity and most dedicatedly, my assertions herefore.

"These are the Words of Enid, to the best of my recollection, on that Fateful day. It was Enid's Declaration that her future Self would fall in love with a Benjamin Webster..."

Again, Sorcha looked up at Ben, who had moved to stand very close by her side.

"I haven't quite decided how I feel about you, you know," she said.

"Well, apparently you figured it out before you told Joseph."

"Or maybe Enid lied to get him to accept what was coming."

Ben looked down and frowned. "Maybe."

Sorcha began reading again.

"...and so I decree that all males descending from me must henceforth bear that name.

"Enid spoke of Bear Talker and Pronounced that his Name and the location of his longhouse shall reveal her to this Benjamin, although the structure in question has long since been demolished.

"Enid gave Warning that someone will attempt to Interfere with my Descendants, who have vowed to protect her. Let it Be Known that if her future self does not pass this very information on to me, I will die in her stead and all my future get will never exist. This is the Crux of my declaration and the Reason all should Heed it.

"In proof of such Otherworldly claims, in her Own hand Enid counseled me on the outcome of events that have yet to happen. Not long after Enid left this world, her words led to my current success in a time when these United States have yet to recognize the Advantages and Validity of my Citizenship. This shall not always be the state of things, as Enid's future self lives in a Society where all are considered Equal and have Equal opportunities."

Sorcha turned the page and there before her was a sheet of paper with hand-written instructions. She recognized Enid's lettering immediately. The words were quite smudged, barely legible even, since the document had been composed on paper with charcoal. She looked up at the portrait on the wall. It was the same kind of paper.

She closed the book and said, "I don't think I should read that."

"I agree," Luanne said. "The paradox is getting a little too convoluted as it is."

Sorcha turned to Ben, who slipped his arms around her.

"Take me home," she said.

Chapter Eighteen

Enid

Bluebird's irritated face came into focus when Enid opened her eyes.

"I thought you would never wake," she said. "The clan will think you lazy."

Enid rolled her head on her sleeping fur and stared past her mother into the gloom of the longhouse. As the revelations laid before Sorcha flooded her memory, tears of sorrow and fright formed and fell.

"Why do you weep?" Bluebird scolded. "You have been given a great honor. Dry your eyes and make haste. James Butler will not tolerate being kept waiting."

With little inflection in her voice, Enid asked, "Do you love me, Mother?"

"What? Why do you ask such things? Are my sacrifices for you not proof enough of my love?"

Enid sniffed and tried to stuff her feelings down where they would not interfere with the things she must accomplish today. "Yes, if you say so."

"I do say so. Now get up."

As Enid dressed, she thought about Paula and Ben, her parents and Grammy Fay. Her heart ached.

Ben had brought her home and by unspoken agreement, he came inside the house and stayed with her. They spent the afternoon on the Internet, again researching the Haudenosaunee people. Sorcha introduced him to her parents, who invited him to dinner. It was a nice evening. Sorcha cherished every little thing her mom and dad said, fighting with all her might to keep her uncertainty from showing. Grammy Fay picked up on it, but Sorcha managed to deflect her questions.

Ben left after dinner, but as soon as Sorcha went into her bedroom for the night, he climbed up the trellis and tapped on her window. She let him in, grateful for his presence. He took off his shoes and jacket and climbed under the covers with her, announcing his plan to hold her all night.

"What if I die when Enid dies?" she asked him. "You can't be here. They'll think you had something to do with it."

"And it'd be true – but you won't die." His arms tightened around her. "Whatever this is, it isn't a big cosmic joke. It can't be. Your existence taught me to believe that things happen for a reason. I think love is a pretty good reason, don't you?"

She tilted her head back and looked at him. "Joseph loves Enid, but that won't save her."

The last thing Sorcha remembered was Ben gently stroking her hair.

Enid followed her mother out into the chill of the morning, wishing she had time to savor the beauty of the sky and the river, but Bluebird hurried her along. When they went past the bathing spot, Enid thought she saw someone's face among the reeds on the far side of the water. Had Joseph found another place to hide? She hoped not. She hoped that wasn't why he was about to get caught.

At the medicine man's wigwam, Bluebird surprised her by declaring her intention to chaperone. "It is unseemly for a young woman to be left alone with a man."

James Butler seemed unfazed by the pronouncement. "As you wish," was all he said.

Enid knew James Butler was defying convention to bring a female on as an apprentice, but he had already demonstrated that he had an open, 'Europeanized' mind. Enid had no idea what to expect the apprenticeship itself to entail. Sorcha's research the afternoon before had delved into the spirituality and superstitions of the tribe. There was plenty of general information out there, but the specifics of what went on behind the walls of the medicine man's dwelling were considered sacrosanct and she'd been unable to find anything on the net. Even in the twenty-first century, Native American people on the whole were reluctant to let outsiders in on their secrets. Sorcha understood, but it frustrated her nonetheless.

As it turned out, James Butler had no plans to reveal anything of importance to Enid – nor did he attempt to grill her for information on the future. Instead, he took advantage of Bluebird's presence and set her to the task of teaching Enid how to weave hemp into rope. They sat cross-legged by the central fire while James Butler read a book by the light of his oil lamp.

The task was mind-numbingly boring, and left Enid longing for a chore that would distract her from her constant thoughts of what was to come.

James Butler was soon called away to attend to an elder who had been struck down by illness. Once they were alone in the wigwam, Bluebird chatted about this and that, finally working her way around to a subject that was clearly important to her. "I know he is not handsome, but you would do well to consider him."

Enid twisted the rough hemp between her fingers and replied matter-of-factly, "I will not live long enough for marriage."

Bluebird's brows came together in a frown. "Why do you speak of such things?"

"Because I know it to be true."

Her mother stared at her. "Can your fate be changed?"

"I wouldn't want it to."

"Why not?" Bluebird was becoming agitated. "If you have the knowledge, use it to your advantage!"

"What if my death were to secure Spotted Fawn's happiness? What then? What if my death is for the greater good? Who is to say the world would be better if I did not bow to my fate?"

Bluebird scrambled to her feet. "I will not listen to more of this."

She stomped out of the wigwam. The moment the door flapped closed, Enid got up and went to James Butler's English desk. She took two sheets of the paper there, folded and tucked them inside her tunic sleeve. She had a stick of charcoal in her hand when the medicine man's voice rang out from the door.

"What do you there?"

Enid turned. Now was not the time to fumble for a plausible lie. Instead, she gestured to the lamp and said, "One day nearly every home in the world will be lit and warmed with electricity, which is lightning from the sky, harnessed."

James Butler was suitably distracted. He drew his thumb and forefinger down the sides of his chin and said, "Tell me, Witch, is the blue spark from rubbing a fur into my hair the same as lightning from the sky?"

Enid nodded and almost laughed when James Butler said, "I knew it!"

"Are you familiar with Benjamin Franklin and his work on the subject?"

James Butler's bulging fish eyes glowed with enthusiasm. "I am not."

"I believe he published his findings, which may be of interest to you. And now, sir, if you would be so kind as to excuse me? I need to…" she trailed off and gave him an apologetic look.

122

"Yes, yes. Go." He stepped aside and she gratefully went outside, holding the charcoal concealed in her hand. Bluebird was nowhere to be seen, and Enid wondered if her chaperonage had come to an end already.

She hurried across the compound and out the palisade. A group of adolescent boys were horsing around at the latrine, shoving each other and laughing. Enid hurriedly ducked into the trees before they saw her. She tried to appear as if she were meandering along in case she was spotted, but she was desperate to see Joseph this one last time.

When she reached his hideout, he grabbed her and pulled her under the hemlock branches, holding a finger to his lips. She froze and sat silently with him. If the raised voices of the boys were any indication, their play had escalated into some kind of confrontation. Despite the danger of being overheard, Enid felt the urgency of her mission and whispered, "I must tell you something very important."

The noises beyond the thicket were retreating. Joseph leaned forward and pulled a branch aside just enough to peer out. He watched for several heartbeats and then turned to her with a question in his eyes.

She pulled the papers from her sleeve, gave him one of them and then snapped the piece of charcoal in half. "I will write a list for you to keep. You must–" her voice broke as she thought of the portrait hanging in the WPS wing of Luanne's college. It was not an image created by a man who felt under pressure to produce it. She changed her approach. "Can you draw?"

He smiled, and it changed his rough features into a face that was almost handsome. She caught her breath and fought the urge to throw herself into his arms. Whatever happened afterward, the list and portrait must come first.

She began to write. Sorcha's knowledge of history had gaps in it a mile wide, but she already knew it was enough to convince Joseph's descendants that she was for real. She warned them about the world wars and the great depression. She jotted down the names of inventions that would change the course of history. Before she knew it, the page was full.

Joseph had been applying charcoal to paper the whole time, occasionally reaching out and grasping her chin to turn her face for his inspection. He was fully immersed in his efforts when she began to talk.

"Don't stop drawing. Let me tell you about my future self."

And she did. The words burst forth like a geyser, all the things he needed to know – all except Sorcha's name and the critical fact that Enid would die before the end of the day. That, she would not tell him. When she got to the part about Ben, he stopped drawing and looked at her with slightly narrowed eyes.

"Are you jealous? That my future self loves another?" It was harder than she expected to see the hurt in his eyes, but he must believe.

"Before you judge me, please know this: Benjamin is a Webster. He is the son of your son, and his son, and so on."

Joseph reached out and put his hand on her knee. He took her list and turned the page over. He wrote, "Are you the mother of my son?"

If a heart were capable of breaking in two, Enid's would have done so after reading those words. The tears she'd somehow managed to suppress broke through and spilled over. He took her face and shook his head, eyes conveying his dismay. He snatched the paper and wrote, "I am sorry."

She laughed through her tears. "Don't be. You did nothing wrong. You have been nothing but a gentleman and – and my hero."

He pulled her into his arms, cradling her until her muffled sobs slowly subsided. She closed her eyes and listened to his breathing, his heart beating steadily under her ear. She felt the stirrings of a longing so intense she wondered if it alone had the power to strike her dead. At that moment, she would have traded anything to remain in his arms forever. But his destiny was entwined with her little sister, a girl that Enid had hardly gotten to know.

"I have a sister in the village. Her name is Spotted Fawn. Will you promise to look after her?"

He leaned back and made a face at her that clearly said, "Why?" His eyes were red rimmed as if he'd been crying, too. She realized now why his eyes reminded her so much of Ben. They were the one feature that persisted through the generations.

She knew, somehow, that now was the time to say goodbye.

"Listen to me. You need to remember everything I've said and keep this list safe. But most importantly, remember that what happens is not your fault, and it *must* happen. Your entire family, everyone who comes from you hereafter, everyone whom you will love, depend upon what happens. Their *lives* depend upon it. Do you understand?"

He shook his head no and took up the charcoal and paper again. He scrawled, "What happens?"

In an echo of the words Ben whispered to Sorcha, she said, "I can't tell you."

He tapped the words "What happens?" with the charcoal insistently.

She slipped from his arms. "Always remember that I loved you."

Before he could stop her, she lurched away, under the branches and out of the thicket. In retrospect, it occurred to her that her headlong flight may have been witnessed by someone, leading them back to Joseph. However he was found, it happened much more quickly than she expected.

No sooner had she gotten back to the longhouse and thrown herself upon her sleeping furs than a disturbance outside prompted her to get back up again.

It was chaos outside. People poured from the longhouses toward the central clearing, where shouting and the high-pitched, repetitive shrieks of warriors could be heard. Enid's heart dropped into her stomach.

The time had come.

She ran, pushing past everyone in her way. Someone fired a musket and she feared she was too late until another shot rang out, fired into the air by a brave near the middle of the square. She shoved and was shoved back as everyone tried to get a closer look. Enid couldn't understand what they were saying, but she didn't need to. They'd found him.

Joseph was on his knees, arms and legs bound and no fewer than three musket barrels resting against his head, which was bloody from whatever beating he'd taken resisting those who'd captured him. Still, he held his head high in defiance. In the dirt nearby was the blanket she'd made him from her skirt. Bluebird had finagled a front-row spot to the spectacle. Enid saw her shouting and shaking her fists at Joseph with the best of them; that is, until her eyes lit upon the blanket. She glanced quickly around before picking it up, and even from where Enid stood on the other side of the clearing, she saw Bluebird's face go slack in shock. From within the blanket, two pieces of paper drifted on the early afternoon breeze. Enid pressed forward against the crowd, but saw that Bluebird caught the pages one by one and clasped them to her breast.

Her mother looked up and met Enid's eyes.

The village elders arrived in all their importance, followed by James Butler in his grotesque mask. He shouted something and the crowd began to quiet.

Enid knew this was her cue, the moment when she would offer her life for Joseph's, but she was frozen to the spot, overcome by a sharp flood of adrenaline that made her violently nauseous. It was only the prospect of watching Joseph die and knowing his death meant there would be no Luanne, no Skip, Sarge or Harry – no Ben to go back to if Sorcha survived – that gave her the strength to move. She pinched the person in front of her and stamped on the next woman's toe, fighting her way to the front where Joseph waited on his fate.

James Butler began to speak in his native tongue. Enid did not have to understand him to know he was accusing Joseph of being a spy and passing judgment upon him. From Sorcha's research, she also knew he was in danger of a quick execution, so she had to act now.

She threw her arms in the air and screamed, a loud, long, warbling screech that ended in wild laughter. James Butler's eyes behind his mask looked astonished. Several braves turned their muskets on her. The crowd was already whipped into a frenzy and it was this mob mentality – and the deeply ingrained superstition of the tribe – that she played upon now.

There were English speakers among those present, and she raised her voice so they could hear. "I am the witch James Butler brought to live among you. It was not he who saved the drowned child, but I." Murmured voices translated to those who didn't understand.

She pointed to James Butler. "Ask him! Ask him if I am a witch! Ask him if I have two spirits! James Butler brought me here to learn from me, but he erred most grievously. For I am a child of two dark spirits."

She pointed to Joseph, "I love this man and ensorcelled him to return my love. He is innocent."

She turned to James Butler. "As you say, medicine man, he was my tool. The only way to release him from my power is to kill me, and after I am dead, if you harm him, my spirits will awaken all of your dead and their spirits will bedevil this tribe forever."

She raised her arms above her head again and shouted, "This man must be released. He must be honored from this day forth and adopted into this tribe."

Enid was no actress, but even she was impressed by her words. She'd composed them while lying in Ben's arms and counted on two things. One, that the Haudenosaunee were a highly spiritual people. Cursing them with retribution from her malicious spirits would be a powerful deterrent. The second thing, and Enid's ace in the hole, was that James Butler would now be aware of her as a threat to his authority. To neutralize her, he would take her up on the offer of an exchange: a life for a life. She didn't know this was how Joseph's life had been spared, but since he had lived on to write the will and witness the birth of the first Benjamin, it had, undeniably, happened.

James Butler had had enough of being upstaged. He said, "You would give your life for this man?"

Enid's chin quivered, but she replied, "You forget, I know what the future holds. This man must not die. You would do well to remember that."

It was a desperate bluff. Whether Joseph lived or died had no bearing on the future of the tribe and no benefit to James Butler himself. But she must have convinced him, because he said loudly, "So be it!"

Several warriors moved toward her, but she cried, "Wait! Please, Medicine Man, have compassion and let me release him from the curse I placed upon him, else he continue to love me after I am gone."

Joseph was struggling violently against his bonds. James Butler hesitated, but then his mask dipped in acknowledgement and she ran forward and dropped to her knees, throwing her arms around Joseph. He was making little mewling sounds that tore her heart out. She pressed her mouth to his ear. "I love you, I love you, never forget. But if you die now, there will be no Ben. I couldn't bear to be alone in both worlds."

His eyes, his eyes…she clung to the memory of his eyes as they dragged her away. Distantly, like a faint reminder of happier days long gone by, she heard her mother calling to her. "E-ee! *Nooo!*"

All day yesterday, Sorcha had tried not to envision how they would do it. A quick, painless death would be best, of course, but it seemed they had something different in mind. She didn't fight as they bound her legs and carried her to the river. They dumped her unceremoniously into a canoe and two braves rowed her to the middle. The crowd lined the shore and she heard them cheer as she was tipped into the frigid water with hardly a splash.

The painful shock of the cold water paralyzed her. Her mother's doeskin dress instantly became sodden and weighed her down. She began to sink. With every ounce of strength within her, she fought the urge to swim upwards. She could do it, she knew she could, even with her ankles bound, but she stared above her at the flickering light of her last day and saw the shadow of the canoe lurking. Surely they would hit her with the hovering paddles if she tried to save herself. The best thing would be to accept it, a prospect that was harder and harder to contemplate as the seconds ticked by and her brain demanded that the depleted air in her lungs be released.

She thought of her father. Would he ever learn of her demise? She thought of Elizabeth and hoped, if there was a heaven, that she was about to see her again.

She felt her body drifting with the swift current. The braves dipped the oars into the water and the canoe began to recede from her vision as they rowed back to shore. Frantically, she tried to swim upward then, but her lungs could take no more. Instinctively, she released a stream of bubbles and inhaled. The agony of the cold water suffusing her lungs was too much. Her back arched and she thrashed futilely as the water suffocated her. Blessed unconsciousness came soon after; her last thought a despairing plea to God or the Creator that the other half of her soul should survive.

Chapter Nineteen

Sorcha

She was choking.

Sorcha arched her back, gagging and struggling against the ropes that bound her.

"Sorch!" An urgent voice pulled her from the void where she fought for her life. She gasped and sat up abruptly, crying out, "*Enid!*"

The ropes were Ben's arms. She turned and clung to him, sucking in air and crying desperately. He held her close, murmuring, "It's okay. You're okay."

A bright light appeared suddenly, and she heard her mother say, "What's wrong? Are you alright?" The concerned words were immediately followed by her father's thundering, "What the hell's going on here? And why is that boy in your bed?"

Her dad didn't wait for anyone to answer. He grabbed the front of Ben's shirt and hauled him across Sorcha's body. Ben didn't resist, but Sorcha wouldn't let go of his arm, "No, Daddy, leave him alone!"

Ben tumbled out of the bed and sprawled on the floor, arm bent back at an awkward angle in Sorcha's determined grip.

"Let go of him, Honey," her mother said, trying to pry Sorcha's fingers open. "You're hysterical."

Grammy Fay appeared in the doorway. She pinched her lower lip and let loose with one of her infamous piercing whistles. Sorcha let go of Ben's arm and he stood, holding his hands out in front of him to try to calm her dad down. "Nothing happened."

"Look at him, Michael," Fay said. "He's fully dressed. They both are."

"I don't care if they're both wearing suits of armor," Michael Sloane responded angrily. "Get out!"

Ben looked at Sorcha, who said woodenly, "She's dead."

"Who's dead?" Amelia Sloane asked.

Sorcha's gaze slid to her grandmother's face. "Enid."

Fay looked horrified. She shook her head and reached for the clock on the bedside table. "Oh, my God. It's two o'clock in the morning. You're awake."

Her mother and father exchanged a look. It was the first time in Sorcha's life that she'd ever woken before morning.

"Well, it's a miracle, but it's beside the point." Her father poked a finger in Ben's chest. "You. Go. Now."

Fay's discerning eyes darted between Ben and Sorcha. She put a hand on Ben's shoulder and said kindly, "I'll take care of her."

Ben nodded, grabbed his jacket and shoes, gave Sorcha one last anguished look and left.

"We'll discuss this in the morning, young lady," her father said.

At the door, her mother produced a tight-lipped smile bereft of warmth. "And prepare yourself for some serious punishment."

Fay ushered her daughter-in-law out and shut the door. Sorcha lay down and immediately began crying again. Fay sat on the edge of the bed and patted her on the back. Sorcha was afraid to fall back asleep; afraid she'd go back to the cold, soundless depths of the river. But when she did drift off, her slumber was deep and dreamless.

Chapter Twenty

Was that music? Sorcha turned her head on the pillow and tried to open her eyes. Her swollen lids resisted, so she was only able to squint at the bright LED display of her alarm clock. The clock had been on the bedside table for as long as she could remember, but the alarm had never been set; there was no reason for it since it wouldn't wake her anyway.

But now it had.

Fay must have set it, must have realized Sorcha would sleep normally because Enid was…gone.

Sorcha's heart squeezed in her chest. Her sore eyes began to burn with the effort to produce still more tears.

She was supposed to get up now and go to school, but how could she act like nothing was wrong? She'd been given one day to grieve for Elizabeth – how many days did it take to get over losing half of yourself?

Enid's life had been filled with hardship and frustration. She'd always compared her lot to Sorcha's and found it wanting. But despite the quality of her existence, she'd still found small joys to cling to. Now even those were gone.

Sorcha sat up and spoke to the empty room. "How many times did you wish you didn't have to live her life?"

She threw the covers off. "Well, guess what, Sorcha? You got your wish."

She went into the bathroom and turned on the shower. "And you're still here, which is better than never waking up again, right?"

She wanted to see Ben. Needed to see him. Needed to look into his eyes and find Joseph there. That was why she forced herself to get up and get ready for the day.

Her parents had left a note on the refrigerator grounding her for a month. It was an apt punishment, from their perspective. They were clueless to the real reason Ben had been with her last night. But Fay knew.

Her grandmother came into the kitchen while Sorcha was eating a bowl of cereal. The bags under her eyes were deeper and darker this morning and Sorcha felt guilty for causing it.

Fay put a hand on Sorcha's head. "How are you, Sweetling?"

"Alive." She fought to suppress a vivid memory of the river.

"Do you want to tell me what happened? Because I'd really like to know."

Sorcha pushed her chair back. "I will. I promise. But right now, I need to get going."

She bundled up and grabbed her backpack. On the porch, Fay's hanging witch startled her by cackling maniacally. It reminded her of Enid's attempt at convincing the Haudenosaunee that she was a crazy witch. It had worked, hadn't it?

She stepped over the roots of the old oak tree, thinking about how Enid had seen the very same tree every day as a sapling. The exhaust from Paula's car drifted through the yard like a ghostly thing.

Luanne and Ben were inside. Sorcha went right into Ben's arms, and to her surprise, Luanne, too, leaned over the seats to join the hug.

"Thank you," Luanne said fervently, rocking her body back and forth. "Thank you."

She sat back and said, "Tell us."

Paula began to drive as Sorcha haltingly told them what had happened. In the middle of the narrative, Luanne interrupted her. "We always wondered what the words 'Are you the mother of my son?' on the back of Enid's list meant."

"He was so confused and hurt," Sorcha said.

Ben squeezed her hand. "He lived and you saved us all."

She nodded and rested her forehead on his shoulder.

When they got to the bus stop, Luanne leaned in. For the first time, she was smiling. "We have a meeting this afternoon. Will you come?"

"I'm grounded. It seems my parents don't approve of me having sleep-overs with boys."

Paula cleared her throat. "What can they do if my car breaks down and you have to walk home? It's Wednesday; Fay'll be in Poughkeepsie, right?"

For the first time, Sorcha noticed Paula had false eyelashes on. "What are you wearing?"

Paula turned her torso and opened her coat to reveal a sparkly black-and-orange-striped t-shirt. "It's Halloween."

"Is it? I'm sorry, I forgot." Every year she and Paula dressed up for school.

"No worries. None whatsoever," Paula replied.

"See you later, then," Luanne said as if everything were settled. She walked away with a bounce in her step.

When they got to school, Sorcha found she didn't want to leave Ben to attend class. She stood next to her locker in the circle of his arms while her fellow students, some costumed, some not, went by.

"You're stronger than you think you are," Ben said. "Carpe diem, okay?"

She nodded, and they parted to go to their respective classes. After History, in the corridor outside her second period class, she saw John. He made a beeline for her and blocked her way.

"Shouldn't you be in jail or something?" she asked.

"For what? Just because I admitted to you privately that it was me who shot at you doesn't mean I'm going to confess."

"Whatever, John. Get out of my way."

"Sure, but first, did Ben ever mention the trust?"

It was clear he was trying to stir up trouble again, but he seemed determined to prevent her from getting to class until she listened, so she snapped, "No. Spit it out."

John shrugged. "You ever wonder why my family was so willing to believe you had two souls just because some crusty old ancestor claimed it was true? It's because Enid's investment advice was never wrong. The WPS made a mint, but the family members couldn't touch any of it. The first Benjamin created a trust that prevented us from profiting from Enid's predictions – at least until she died. Wanna guess how much money Ben's about to get for making sure Enid sacrificed herself?"

Even if her throat hadn't closed up in shock and dismay, Sorcha wouldn't have given John the satisfaction of a response. She pushed past him and went to class, sitting in her seat and opening her book like an automaton. It never occurred to her that John's words weren't true, since they made complete and total sense. It had nagged and nagged at her that these people were such ardent believers of something that was not just improbable, but preposterous, really. Her own parents had not believed her, so why would an entire family devote themselves to the legend of her for two hundred years?

She remembered a phrase from Joseph's will, "Not long after Enid left this world, her words led to my current success in a time when these United States have yet to recognize the Advantages and Validity of my Citizenship." Enid had written down all the future events she could think of, including inventions that anyone in the know would have been wise to invest in.

She'd never intended for it to be 'investment advice,' as John put it, but that's what her words had become.

By the time lunch crawled around, she was not just angry; she was frustrated with herself for not having considered all the consequences of her own actions. She was the one who had so blithely given Joseph the 'investment advice' in the first place, so how could she justify getting angry? And yet angry she was.

She and Paula sat on the stage in their usual spot. Sorcha didn't touch the lunch Grammy Fay had packed for her. She just sat on the linoleum like it was her launch pad and she was a tightly coiled spring.

"You okay?" Paula asked. "I mean, obviously you're not okay, but you seem…I don't know, more wound up than I expected."

Sorcha glanced over to where John was sitting with his friends. She'd never seen him in the gym at lunch before. On any given day, he probably left campus to buy fast food and smoke. He wasn't disguising the fact that he was watching her. Every once in a while, he looked around, and she knew he was waiting for Ben to make an appearance so he could witness the fireworks.

Ben was late. She wondered if he'd left school early to go cash his check.

"Sorch?"

"Sorry. Um…wound up…yeah, you could say that."

She saw Ben then, coming through the door with none other than Dalton Boyle. The two walked companionably up the aisle and stopped in front of Paula and Sorcha.

"Hey, Paula," Dalton said. "Nice costume." He didn't even look at Sorcha.

As much as she was itching to let Ben have it, Sorcha held her tongue. Dalton was making his move and not even Ben's well-deserved comeuppance could prompt Sorcha to ruin it for her best friend. Paula had been nothing but loyal and deserved to be happy.

Still, Sorcha couldn't fake a pleasant expression. Ben stepped close to the edge of the stage but didn't touch her. Was he already pulling away now that he'd gotten what he wanted?

Paula and Dalton were bantering back and forth, but Sorcha only heard every third word or so. Her resentment simmered just under the surface and some of it must have showed because Ben said quietly, "If you want to leave, we could go for a walk or something."

A walk. Yes. That way, she could tell him what was on her mind without ruining Paula's big moment and without giving John the satisfaction of savoring the effect his words had on her.

133

She jumped off the stage and walked up the aisle and out the door without looking to see if Ben followed. She headed straight for the exit, but from behind she heard him say, "Shouldn't we get our coats?"

Without turning, she said, "Oh, I'm plenty warm, thank you."

He grabbed her arm. "Wait. Are you mad at me?"

She looked down at his hand. "If you want to keep that hand, I suggest you let go of me."

He released her arm and said in a low voice, "John got to you, didn't he?"

She glared at him. "Just out of curiosity, what excuse were you planning on using?"

"I'm going to turn down the money."

Her mouth dropped open. "What?"

"You think I want you to wonder how I really feel? No amount of money would be worth that."

She pressed a fist tightly to her chest, touched that he was willing to give up so much to prove how he felt. But she said, "That's stupid."

Now it was Ben's turn to say, "What?"

She dropped her head and put her hands over her face as all the hurt and confusion slowly drained away. When she looked up again, he was waiting patiently.

"You should have told me," she said.

"I wanted to. It's just...the money clouded things, you know? If you'd known, you might have thought..."

"Thought the money was more important than the fact that if Enid didn't die, you wouldn't have been born? You didn't have a lot of faith in me, did you?"

He put a hand to her cheek and whispered, "I had all the faith in the world."

When she didn't respond, his hand dropped to his side. He stood there like a man waiting for judgment to be passed.

Over his shoulder, she saw John enter the hallway and stop abruptly when he caught sight of them. He crossed his arms and leaned casually against a bank of lockers, not hiding the fact that he was watching and listening.

"I want you to take the money," she said, loudly enough for John to hear.

Ben's left eyebrow disappeared into the lock of hair on his forehead. "Why?"

"Because you need a car. I don't particularly like riding around on your handlebars. Hurts my butt."

She slipped her arms around his waist, pressed herself against him and lifted her face. It started out as a way to show John his latest attempt to stir up trouble had failed, but as Ben took the hint and met her lips with his, she forgot about everything but how alive she felt in his arms.

Chapter Twenty-one

Luanne picked Ben and Sorcha up in her brand-new pickup truck. She proudly drove to the opening in the gate that led to the path along the highway. Someone had torn down a bigger section of the fence, and Luanne drove up over the curb and onto the path.

"Don't worry. We couldn't say anything before, but this is WPS land."

Dozens of cars and trucks lined the field that surrounded the copse of trees where Bear Talker's longhouse used to be.

The first time Sorcha had attended a WPS meeting, the mood had been festive. Now it was nothing short of jubilant. When she appeared in the circle hand-in-hand with Ben, a ragged cheer rose up, startling the birds from the trees. Everyone was grinning and clapping each other on the back. Even the sunshine seemed to agree it was a worthy day to send its rays down upon them. Each happy face only sobered long enough to wish Sorcha well and to express, in one form or another, how sorry they were that Enid had died. A few of them had the temerity to ask her what it felt like, and to them she replied, "Someday you'll know."

She finally had the opportunity to meet Sarge, a big man with the enlarged and reddened nose of a chronic alcoholic, who pumped her hand up and down and boomed, "Damned glad to meet you, girl."

Paula hadn't come along. She and Dalton had made plans to go see a movie. "I'll tell my mom my car wouldn't start just in case she talks to your mom, okay?"

"Have fun tonight. Don't, uh, do anything I wouldn't do," Sorcha said.

"When you get off from being grounded, we can double-date."

Sorcha hoped by then the idea would appeal to her more. It was hard to summon the proper enthusiasm while the wound from losing Enid was still so fresh.

136

It was hard, in fact, to listen to the Webster family celebrate. Someone had set up tables and a portable grill and the smell of cooking meat reached her. She hadn't eaten her lunch, but the scent failed to stimulate her appetite. Still, when someone brought her a plate heaped high with charred chicken and beans, she nibbled at it before abandoning it on one of the tables.

Ben was glued to her side. "This is too much, too soon, isn't it?"

She looked around. Children, absent from the first meeting, shouted and laughed and ran around. "No, I'm glad I got to see this."

Sarge stepped up onto a plastic chair and raised his arms for silence. The adults closest to him began to shush those around them, and silence moved through the crowd like a ripple in still water. Sarge's arms slowly lowered and he spread them expansively, as if inviting everyone there to come give him a hug.

"Two hundred and thirty some-odd years ago," he said, his deep voice projecting across the clearing with seemingly little effort, "an old Mahican medicine man lived on this very spot. His name was Bear Talker and his nephew was Joseph Webster."

Murmurs of appreciation spread through the crowd.

Ben linked his fingers with Sorcha's.

"One cold fall day," Sarge said, "Joseph met a young woman named Enid who would change his destiny. When a party of Mohawk warriors met with Bear Talker, they came under the pretense of peace. But Bear Talker was suspicious and sent Joseph on a false errand in case the Mohawk were lying. It turned out they did have an ulterior motive, and when Bear Talker refused to tell them where to find Enid, they tortured him."

Sorcha gasped and looked up at Ben. He squeezed her hand.

Sarge continued. "Joseph came back from the errand to find his uncle's longhouse engulfed in a raging conflagration. He was too late to help Bear Talker, whose last words to him were, 'Save her.' And so Joseph rode his horse through the fields and arrived at Enid's house before the Mohawk."

"I didn't know," Sorcha whispered. "Poor Bear Talker."

"But Joseph didn't save her," Sarge said, his voice full of sadness. His eyes briefly met Sorcha's. He didn't have to say it: the reason Joseph didn't save Enid, couldn't save her, was because she fell asleep.

"Instead," Sarge's voice boomed out, "the Mohawk caught them, and they cut out his tongue to silence him. When Joseph was lying staked to the ground, choking on his own blood, he vowed to find her. Soon after the Mohawk took her away, the household slaves came out of hiding and

137

released him from his bonds. Joseph barely allowed them to tend to his wounds before he set out."

Sorcha remembered the crude stitches to the base of Joseph's tongue and sent up a silent prayer of thanks to Bess and Aggie. It was good to know they had survived.

"The Mohawk were easy to track. Joseph followed them to a large Haudenosaunee village. On the outskirts, he released his horse and snuck as close to the village as possible. But his thirst for revenge was not strong enough to overcome his injuries. He might have died there, hidden away so near to his goal of carrying out his uncle's final wish."

Sarge smiled then, his cheeks contracting in dimples very much like Ben's. "But don't despair! Because Enid..." he looked at Sorcha with raised eyebrows and mouthed the word, 'you,' before going on, "Because Enid found him and nursed him back to health, and he found a better reason than revenge to go on."

Several people in the crowd said, "Love."

"Love!" Sarge shouted. Then more quietly, "Love. And it was this love that made it possible for our family to not just survive the last two-hundred and thirty some-odd years, but to exist. If it were not for Sorcha, who stands before us less than a day after dying, after giving up half of herself...for love...we, every single one of us standing here on this glorious day, would have winked out of existence without any evidence that we had ever walked the Creator's earth."

Sorcha had been so caught up in Sarge's speech it startled her when Ben leaned down and said quietly in her ear, "See? I told you he had charisma."

She laughed self-consciously. "He's got everyone in the palm of his hand, hasn't he?"

But Sarge wasn't finished yet. "There is nothing we can do or say to convey the depth of our gratitude. And there's no way we can make it up to you: the loss of Enid. How could we? Still, thanks to you, Joseph had a lifetime to think about it, and I know this is the last thing you may have expected, Sorcha, but he made sure your investment advice would benefit you, too."

Sorcha looked at him, appalled.

Sarge said quickly, "That's not to say he thought money would in any way compensate you. He wasn't one to put a price on life, none of us are."

Sorcha's eyes found John, who lurked on the fringes of the group, just as Harry had at the last meeting. He shrugged and gave her a crooked smile, as if to say, "Not all of us, anyway."

"And with these final words of heartfelt gratitude to you, Sorcha, I hereby declare the Webster Protection Society dissolved!"

A deafening "Hurrah!" rose from the crowd, and to Sorcha's surprise everyone around her set off little hand-held confetti cannons. Bits of sparkling paper rained down like brightly colored snow.

The merriment got a little crazier after that. Skip brought out a case of champagne and corks began popping. Someone handed Sorcha a plastic champagne glass brimming with the clear bubbly liquid. She sipped it once to be polite, immediately disliking the taste. It ended up next to the discarded plate of food.

Ben must have seen the glazed look in her eye, because he gently steered her away from the frenzy to the tree he'd sat under that first day. He knelt down and gave her the same expectant look he'd given her then. She laughed and sat within the circle of his arm. They watched the Webster family celebrate their good fortune.

It had never occurred to Sorcha that they would give her any portion of the money. She didn't want to think about it now, didn't want to sully Enid's memory with thoughts of what her life had been worth.

It did make her think about how the lives of these people would change. Not only had the specter of their sudden demise disappeared, but their money worries were gone as well. But everyone knew money didn't guarantee happiness. It wouldn't bring back Ben's father, whose loss had been the catalyst for Ben going to juvie, and had sent his uncle Harry into homeless seclusion.

She scanned the crowd until she spotted Harry, talking with Luanne not far away.

Sorcha looked at Ben. "Harry is John's real father, isn't he?"

Ben took in a breath before saying, "How'd you guess?"

"Process of elimination. I think if he were your brother, you'd treat him differently, so it couldn't have been your father. He's not Sarge's son, and Skip's not the kind of guy to sleep with his brother's wife."

Ben laughed. "Well, I don't know about that, but yeah, from what I understand, Harry's the culprit. Um, speak of the devil…" Ben nudged her and nodded.

She turned. Luanne was leading Harry by the arm, tugging the coarsely dressed man in their direction. Luanne looked excited, and not just in response to the general merriment, but as if she had discovered something.

When Sorcha saw the tissue paper charcoal rub of the words on Sarah Murphy's gravestone in Harry's rough-skinned hands, she caught her breath. Ben helped her up and she brushed her fingers down the seat of her pants to remove the dirt and leaves.

"You are not going to believe this!" Luanne was practically shouting. She pushed Harry forward. "Go on, tell them. Tell them what it says."

The people in the vicinity quieted down to hear. Harry lifted the tissue, made a phlegmy sound, like a harrumph, and read, "One Soul Becomes Two."

Sorcha blinked. Her lips moved as she silently repeated the words. As their meaning struck her, she turned to Ben and cried out, "Enid!"

Ben's face was alight with the same wonder she felt. He swept her off her feet and swung her in a dizzying circle. She bent her head back and gazed up at the tops of the trees as they spun around, the weight on her soul lifting with each beat of her heart.

Epilogue

A white shaft of sunlight slanted in through the wavy window glass. Her eyes focused on myriad tiny dust motes floating lazily in the cold air of the small, unfamiliar room. She'd awakened from a deep, black nothingness some time ago and tried to get up but had been overcome with dizziness and nausea. Now she waited in the strange bed for someone to come.

When the door finally opened, a man brought in a tray and set it on a chest by the bed. He appeared to be older than her by several years, dressed in plain homespun, dark hair pulled into a stub of a ponytail under a tricorn hat.

"Good, yer awake," he said, removing the hat. "Do ya speak English?"

She realized he thought she was Native American. "I am English…I mean American."

"Ah. Well, ye'll forgive me if I assumed otherwise. Ya were dressed like a native and living among them. Name's Charles Murphy. How do ya feel?"

"Alive?" She hadn't meant for the word to come out as a question.

He laughed. "And just barely, at that. What's yer name?"

"Did you…did you rescue me?"

"Aye." He looked down at the hat in his hands. "And me captain weren't none too happy when I brought a half-drowned chit back ta the garrison."

"I am sorry to have caused you any trouble." She sat up. The dizziness was still present, but milder. At the moment, the hunger pangs gnawing at her stomach were more urgent. Without waiting for an invitation, she reached out and took a hunk of bread from the tray. It was stale and tasted as if the cook had added no salt, but it was food.

"Oh, please," he said, gesturing to the bread in her hand. "You must be…"

141

He seemed more flustered than a man who'd forgotten his manners should be. She noticed him staring in the vicinity of her chest and glanced down. The buckskin dress was gone, and she was wearing a man's shirt. It was so big the neckline hung halfway off her shoulder. She tugged on it and looked up into his red face. He had pale, lightly freckled skin and green eyes, like Sorcha's.

"How did you rescue me? The last thing I remember was..." she trailed off as the horrific memory of dying in the cold sparkling water assailed her.

The corners of Charles Murphy's lips turned down. "Truth be told, me patrol had been watchin' the village fer days. The current brought yer body right to us. I saw ya save that child and it struck me that yer method was sound. Who would have figured I'd have the opportunity to use it on ya?"

Who indeed? She finished chewing and reached for a tankard that turned out to be filled with milk. It was warm, and unlike the bread, fresh. After gulping half of it down, she cradled the tankard in her hands and stared into it self-consciously. She wanted to ask him who had dressed her but decided against it. Something about the way he looked at her, like he knew her intimately, told her all she needed to know.

As if he could read her thoughts, he said, "I, uh, took no liberties, Miss. All the men in me patrol are respectful."

To hide her embarrassment, she took another bite of the stale bread.

"Beggin' yer pardon, Miss, but I do need ta know yer name. We'll be wanting ta contact yer people."

She chewed slowly to delay her answer, looking up into Charles Murphy's earnest face. When she finally replied, her words were softly spoken, but filled with determination.

"I have no people. My name is...Sarah."

The end.

www.ingramcontent.com/pod-product-compliance
Lightning Source LLC
Chambersburg PA
CBHW061246170626
46809CB00007B/2864